THE LIFE OF
DAVID GALE

THE LIFE OF DAVID GALE

A NOVEL BY
Dewey Gram

BASED ON THE MOTION PICTURE SCREENPLAY BY
Charles Randolph

AN ONYX BOOK

Prologue

Fog smothered the early-evening sounds in the East Texas scrublands outside Huntsville.

No visitors disturbed the silence of the small cemetery. It was a dirt-poor burial field, nearly grassless, set a good way back from the highway behind tall pines and sagging split-rail fencing. The graves were untended. The grave markers—identical, rough-made, white wooden crosses—bore no names, numbers only: serial numbers, dates of death. TEXAS DEPARTMENT OF CORRECTIONS CEMETERY, announced the plain-lettered wooden sign at the graveled entrance turnoff from the highway. It was the disposal ground for prisoners who died in custody—the unlucky. The unlucky and unclaimed. Outcasts a final time.

Across the field, a rust-red mass with guard towers and razor wire rose out of the fog.

Sundowner birdcalls drifted faintly across the terrain. Distant yard dogs set up a flurry of yapping.

On the outskirts of town, someone was passing, setting them off.

The foggy road was deserted, though. It was dinnertime and nobody was out on the two-lane county blacktop, a strange lull on the ordinarily busy highway splitting the parched, stubbled farmland. It was as though everybody were already there—already where they were going for the evening. Or they were not going at all.

A rental car sat abandoned on the side of the road. The driver's-side door stood open, and smoke spewed from under the raised hood. A mile farther on, nearly to town, a woman breathing heavily raced along the shoulder.

She ran as though her life depended on it. She faltered, out of breath, then immediately picked up her stride again, pushing herself in a frantic effort to will her legs and lungs past their limits.

Across the brown fields, a mile-long goods train rolled along slowly, seeming to keep pace with her.

She crossed the line into the small Texas town, sprinting along the street in her low-heeled work shoes, not slackening her speed. A car came out of the fog behind her. She turned to wave it down; the driver blared the horn, swerved around her, and sped on.

Disheveled and perspiring, desperate, she ran through the outlying neighborhoods of the town, carrying in her hand a videocassette. The sounds of her breathing and her shoes hitting the pavement echoed in the muggy, misty air. Of the few townsfolk she passed, none seemed to notice her.

She ran and ran, the cassette in her grasp like a message from Marathon signaling the fate of the battle. Past the feed store, the railroad, the Tabernacle of God, the nail salon, the minimart, the check-cashing outlet.

She heard an uproar in the distance, fading in and out—human voices, chanting.

Chapter 1

Barbara Kruger was a smart, rough-talking, profane woman with none of the buttoned-up reticence of her white, Ivy League journalist colleagues.

Kruger had cut her teeth as a youth and community-relations—read "crime and gangs"—reporter on a black weekly in Baltimore. Three years later she jumped to the police beat at the *Baltimore Sun*. You don't survive as a police reporter in Baltimore unless you learn fast how to be the real thing: as tough as any of the cops, as mean as the crooks, more persistent and demanding than either of them in going after the actual story, not just the "on the record" version.

She was nominated for a Pulitzer for a series on dope rings operated by security rent-a-cops in public junior high schools. It got her noticed. The *Washington Post* hired her away from the *Sun* to do, it turned out, "ghetto features"—minority lifestyle stories—for the style section. Kruger reported them and wrote them, but she didn't relish them as a steady diet. Too soft.

Just at the right time, *NEWS Magazine* in New York

made her an offer to come on board as a law and criminal justice writer-editor for their back-of-the-book section and a contributor on big crime stories in the nation section. She made the move to New York and into the somewhat less harried, relatively posh life of a newsweekly journalist, but she came with serious reservations. She warned the editor at *NEWS Magazine* that she wouldn't hew to any party line and that she was no Establishment mouthpiece. They both agreed she probably wouldn't last a year, but she would try it.

Four years later she was head of the section and an associate editor of the magazine. Now, eight years further along, at age forty-seven, she sat glued to the TV in her office, a short, overweight workaholic boss-woman wearing an old jogging suit and new, oversized athletic shoes, stuffing low-fat tortilla chips into her mouth without looking. BARBARA D. KRUGER, CRIME AND PUNISHMENT EDITOR, said the nameplate on her desk. She had half-frame granny glasses on a cord around her neck and one chunky leg up on her messy desk, massaging her bum knee with an electric massager. *NEWS Magazine* covers reporting the decade's big crimes and trials—her cover stories—lined the walls.

On the television, a CNN reporter, A. J. Roberts, stood on the steps in front of the U.S. Supreme Court building. "The high court also refused to stay Friday's execution of former philosophy professor David Gale," Roberts said.

"Christ doin' karaoke," Kruger said with her mouth full.

"Gale had sought a review of his 1994 conviction for the rape and murder of his University of Texas colleague Constance Harraway," Roberts continued.

Kruger reached for a phone, hit four numbers, stuffed in another chip.

A book jacket photo of Constance flashed on the screen.

"The case has received nationwide media attention," Roberts said, "because Gale and Harraway were activists for DeathWatch, a nonprofit, anti–death penalty group based in Austin . . ."

Kruger waited impatiently on the phone, munching, swallowing, as she listened to Roberts's report.

"Defense lawyers had hoped to argue that Gale's former activism against capital punishment unduly prejudiced the Texas judicial system," Roberts said. "Citing 'discriminating purpose' . . ."

"Hey, they're not gonna stay Gale," Kruger said into the phone. "It's on CNN right now. Listen . . ." She held the phone out in the direction of the TV, using the opportunity to eat another chip.

As old footage of David Gale on a talk show rolled across the screen, Roberts went on: "Citing 'discriminating purpose,' the defense pointed to the State of Texas's 'clear political gain' in executing its leading opponent of the death penalty . . ."

Inserts of old black-and-white photos of Gale as a political activist for various other causes flashed up on the screen: Gale sitting on a stage with a group of scientists concerned about Global Warming, Gale speaking to students protesting at the World Economic Summit, Gale standing at a photo op with a group of pro–gun control Congressmen on the steps of the Capitol in Washington.

"The deal was Bitsey would get the interview if the stay was refused," Kruger said into the phone, finally swallowing. She downed another chip as she listened. "He'll talk to her for two hours a day. Tuesday, Wednesday, and Thursday . . . Can't do a Friday . . . No . . . 'Cause Friday is the day they execute him . . . The lawyer said only Bitsey."

"They had also hoped to argue before the nine Justices that the sentencing court further failed to consider," Roberts said on TV, "that the victim was herself an abolitionist activist who would most assuredly have protested her own murderer's execution. . . ."

"Only Bitsey means only Bitsey," Kruger said into the phone. "I don't get to make the rules, Bill. I'm a fat black woman."

Bitsey Bloom walked in Kruger's office. "What we *need* is to put her on a plane to Texas," Kruger barked into the phone.

"Gale's going down," Bitsey said.

Kruger shushed her with a we-already-know gesture.

"Why do you always get lordosis around legal?" Kruger said into the phone. "Hold on." She put the phone on hold, dropped it on a pile of papers on the desk, grabbed the bag of chips, and was out the door. Bitsey followed her.

They walked catty-corner across the busy and buzzing open editorial floor of *NEWS Magazine* toward another office.

"What's lordosis?" Bitsey said.

Bitsey was an attractive, young-but-not-too-young woman. She purposely marginalized her youth and looks with a severe brush-back of her light brown hair and minimal makeup. She wore, as always, a suit that was expensively cut, businesslike but fashionable, and, as always, elegant but practical half-heel pumps. The whole look said, "Take me seriously or lose your balls," and had the effect of making her age hard to determine. In a certain light she looked shy of thirty; at other times, old enough to have done a thousand stories and heard it all.

Bitsey had contemplated, when she became a journalist, dropping the nickname Bitsey in favor of her given name, Elizabeth. But she decided against it. If Bitsey had been good enough for Bryn Mawr, two years in the Peace Corps in Malaysia, and a fellowship at the Kennedy School of International Affairs getting a master's in political science—and by the way, if Buffy was good enough for Buffy Chandler, who owned and ran the *L.A. Times*, and Jimmy was good enough for the good ole boy who had become president—then, to hell with it, Bitsey Bloom would do for her professional name and byline.

They entered the second, bigger *NEWS Magazine* office, which featured a NATIONAL EDITOR brass nameplate in a tasteful Bodoni font on the open door.

Bill Mullarkey, a hound dog–faced, bow-tied Yale man in his shirtsleeves sat at his overly neat desk, still holding on the phone. Kruger and Bitsey entered, and he hung up the phone with a mild roll of the eyes.

"Lordosis," Bill said, correcting her pronunciation. He walked over and closed the office door.

"What is lordosis?" Bitsey said.

"Female ape's posture when preparing to get screwed," Kruger said.

Bitsey shot Kruger a look.

Bill adopted his Waspy, lockjawed paternal tone. "Look, kids," he said, "setting aside the cost issue— though half a million dollars for three days of interviews is not only illegal, it's obscene. . . ."

"Market value," Kruger said. "The guy's never

talked." It was common knowledge in their world that *Time*, *Newsweek*, and *U.S. News*—not to mention *People*, *US Magazine*, and the *National Enquirer*—had firm offers out to Gale if he'd agree to a tell-all interview. Network and cable news wanted to walk the last mile with him too, but he had not responded to any offer. Instead, through his lawyer, he had sought out contact with Bitsey.

"That aside," Bill said, "I—we—are still uncomfortable with the arrangement." He put one of his big cordovan-shod hooves up on the wastebasket—he was one of the few journalist-dinosaurs around who still favored the wingtip banker look.

"Uncomfortable?" Bitsey said.

"You've just spent a very public seven days in jail," he said, "for a very public contempt-of-court citation."

"Protecting sources, even kiddie-porn scum," Bitsey said, "is magazine policy. If you were so goddamn uncomfortable with the story, why did you slap it on both the domestic and international covers?"

"Bitsey," Bill said with a dry look, "your Pulitzer chasing by any means necessary is a separate conversation." Bill, with his cool rimless eyeglasses and $300 Turnbull & Asser shirts, was a grand master of condescension. It came with the background: Greenwich, Connecticut, boyhood; Choate before Yale; Columbia Law after Yale ("Did I mention I went to school in New Haven?"); newsmagazine bureau stints in Chicago, Saigon, and Paris; elevation to nation editor at age forty-three. He was a prince of the realm and didn't pretend to be anything but.

"What makes me—us—uncomfortable here," he

said, "is the fact that a rapist-slash-murderer has asked to spend the last three days of his life giving an interview—his very first—to a reporter who is now famous for protecting sexual deviants. A reporter who is also a very attractive woman . . ."

Bitsey and Kruger groaned in perfect unison, without even having to look at each other.

"This is disparate treatment," Kruger said matter-of-factly.

"I could go if I were an ugly, chatty guy?" Bitsey said.

Bill gave a begrudging half smile. "There's an agenda issue here," he said, "which would be diffused with the presence of a male. . . ."

"I hear lawyers gleefully saying the words: 'Bloom vs. NEWS Magazine Inc.,'" Kruger said, nodding knowingly to Bitsey, who nodded knowingly back.

"'Well, Your Honor,'" Bitsey said, "'I started to notice that my assignments were being determined on the basis of my sex.'"

Bill stared at the wall above their heads, waiting out the feminist-legal broadside—which he had fully expected.

"You've gotta let her go now," Kruger said to Bill with a satisfied smile.

"That's not quite what I meant," Bill said.

"He's gotta let you go," Kruger said to Bitsey. They both smiled. Kruger turned and opened the door.

"'Certain references were made,'" Bitsey said.

"All right. All right. Enough," Bill said. He looked at Kruger, then at Bitsey. "The intern will be with you at all times?"

"Yes," Kruger said. She pulled Bitsey out the door

before Bill could change his mind or Bitsey could step in it and foul it up.

Kruger and Bitsey came out of Bill's office. They passed by a bank of eight TVs tuned to network, cable, and local news programs.

"Intern?" Bitsey blurted. "No. You've got to be kidding, Kruger. I'm not baby-sitting."

Kruger gave no answer but her famous Cheshire cat smile. She was lit up. This would work. She'd gotten her way. She'd managed to convince the Wallendas—so the top editors were called—to agree to an unusual dollar-and-publication arrangement for what her reporter's instinct told her would be well worth the candle: a unique and possibly politically loaded story. Maybe she'd turn out to be wrong; maybe it would be a fizzle. But she didn't think so. This one had all the earmarks—a strange saga built around hot-button issues that promised to reveal not just an unusual set of facts and events but maybe some secrets of the human heart, too.

Chapter 2

They picked up a rental car at the Dallas–Fort Worth
Airport and got on Texas Interstate 45 just outside
the airport heading south. It was well after sundown,
but still thickly humid and as hot as only Texas
nights can be.

Zack Stemmons sat in the passenger seat, smoking
and looking at a case file in his lap. He held the
cigarette just outside the slightly open window. Zack
was a skinny, floppy-haired twenty-six-year-old with
ambitiously hip chin fuzz that was meant to lend
an air of cosmopolitan experience and authority. He
looked like a disheveled student. Nonetheless, he did
give off a sense of being a bright and willing fellow traveler.

As Bitsey drove, she kept checking the dashboard's
instrument panel. Tapping the panel, flicking her
eyes from the road to the dial, she said with strained
patience, "Gale's DNA was everywhere. His semen
was inside her." The car's headlights moved past a
sign: HUNTSVILLE 27 MILES. "He was seen leaving her
house," she said. "His prints were all over the
kitchen, including one on the bag."

Zack held a black-and-white police crime-scene photo up to the light: a woman, naked on a kitchen floor, hands cuffed around her. Covering her head was an opaque white plastic bag, sealed around the neck with duct tape. Bitsey glanced over at it and looked quickly away.

"Half a thumbprint," he said.

"Okay, half a thumbprint," she said. "That's enough."

"He could have touched it before it was a murder weapon," he said.

"Do you fondle your friends' garbage bags?" she said.

"Yeah, I get very touchy around household plastics," Zack said. "I'm particularly fond of Tupperware."

"Tupperware?" she said, keeping the car in the far-right lane, watching the heat gauge.

"Look," Zack said. "I'm just saying, the bag could have been sitting out on the counter or something."

She took her eyes off the road and looked at him for a beat. "Hey, Zack?" she said.

"Yeah," he said.

"He did it," she said. "Now he's gonna die. And you know something? Maybe that's exactly what he deserves." She went back to keeping her eyes on the road and on the occasional pairs of headlights zipping past going the other way.

"But the murder's way too fucking clumsy," Zack said, shuffling through the file. "This guy's a major intellectual. Top of his Yale class, a Rhodes scholar, tenured at twenty-seven, two books published. He's an academic stud."

Zack picked up another photo from the file and

examined it: a Christmas shot of the Gale family in front of a large, decorated hearth: David at age thirty-four; his beautiful wife, Sharon, in her late twenties; and son, Jamie, age six, beaming over an armload of Christmas loot.

"Look at his wife—she's a regular Grace Kelly," Zack said. "Old money svelte. Her father was ambassador to Spain. . . ."

"Shit!" Bitsey said, looking at the instrument panel. "The light's on again." She slowed the car. Two cars beeped in annoyance and sped past her.

"Ignore it," Zack said. "It's a rental."

"Thanks for the tip, Zack," Bitsey said. "Do you smell anything?"

"No," Zack said. "Besides, the guy's a flaming liberal."

Bitsey looked down at the now-flickering overheat light. "A person's politics has nothing to do with their propensity to commit a crime," she said. "Aren't we supposed to smell something if it's overheating?"

"Wrong, seventy-three percent of all serial killers vote Republican," Zack said.

"Throw the cigarette out so we can smell," Bitsey said.

Zack reached toward the car ashtray.

"No!" Bitsey said. "You'll stink up the car. Throw it out!"

Zack recoiled at her vehemence. "I'm not gonna fucking pollute," he said with mock outrage.

"Zack!" Bitsey said. She realized she was sounding like her own mother, and she didn't like it. It was Zack's fault. And Kruger's. Why wouldn't they just let her do this her standard way: alone?

Zack pinched off the cherry and what was left of the tobacco and let it drop out the window. He held up the filter that remained in his fingers and showily put it in the ashtray. She gave him a look. They rode in silence.

Cars continued to overtake and pass them as Bitsey nursed the car along at granny speed. She sniffed again. "We'd better stop," she said. "Shit, this is so irritating."

"How far to Huntsville?" Zack said, leaning over to look at the gauge. He was beginning to smell something.

"Look, I'll pull off. . . ." Bitsey said. She pointed to an approaching rest area EXIT sign. They shared a glance, then a laugh.

Zack affected an evil, maniacal cackle. "*NEWS Magazine* reporters Bitsey Bloom and Zack Stemmons entered the rest area with car trouble," he said, in a *Hard Copy* announcer voice.

Bitsey took the exit for the rest area. It was lighted, but not very well. There were no other cars or trucks there, and almost no amenities. A cinderblock building housed toilets, but that was all—not even a coffee or Coke machine. And not even a pay phone on a post for emergencies.

"But," Zack continued in his tabloid voice, "it wasn't just their car that was in trouble." He scatted a few bars of scary music.

"*I'm* a reporter," Bitsey said. "You're an intern." She'd better nip any pretensions in the bud, she thought, even at the cost of coming off as a hard-ass.

"Whatever," Zack said, with an exaggerated roll of the eyes.

Bitsey pulled the small rental sedan into a parking

space and cut the engine. She made sure to park under a light. Cars whizzed by on the highway.

She searched under the dash, found the release and popped the hood. They got out, raised the hood, and stood looking at the radiator, both sniffing. The telltale odor of escaping radiator fluid wafted up to them.

"Is it hot?" Bitsey said.

Zack reflexively reached out and put his hand on it. "Ow!" he said. "Jesus, yes. Isn't it always?"

Bitsey shrugged.

"So what do I do?" Zack said. He looked at his singed hand, feeling like an idiot.

"Call the office and have someone on overnight get the rental road-service number," Bitsey said.

Zack took out his phone and dialed. He made a face. "No service," he said. He looked around, hoping for a pay phone.

"Goddamn it," Bitsey said. In her whole career, she had never missed a plane, an interview, or a deadline when on a story. Infamous were the stories of reporters who had taken wrong turns on the road, gotten ignominiously lost, and blown the assignment. She knew several who had accidentally rushed onto the wrong plane or train and missed the action entirely. One colleague at *NEWS Magazine* ended up in Mexico City instead of Albuquerque and couldn't get back until past deadline. Another had his rental car freeze solid under him in the Canadian far north, preventing his filing in time. The rental car, not retrieved until spring, was a big-ticket expense account item.

"I've gotta pee," Zack said.

Bitsey continued to glare at the engine.

Zack moved toward the unlighted toilet building. He hesitated at the door. It was smelly and dark inside as well as out. Scary dark. He decided to use the side of the building.

Bitsey watched headlights coming toward her in the mist. "We've got company," she said, then realized that Zack wasn't there. "Zack!" she said.

A large gray pickup truck approached. The driver's cowboy hat was ominously silhouetted through the windshield. He slowed to a stop several dozen yards short of where Bitsey was standing and let the pickup idle. The driver wore a Stetson and a ranch jacket. The part of his face that was visible was weatherbeaten but not old. He and Bitsey exchanged a look.

"Zack!" Bitsey called.

Zack appeared at her side. "Yeah?" he said.

The cowboy registered Zack. He gave both them and their car a casual look, put the pickup into gear, and pulled away and back onto the highway. They watched him go. Creepy.

Or was it? They both knew there was nothing unusual about a man in a pickup on the Texas byroads. Every third vehicle they had seen since leaving the Dallas–Fort Worth airport was a pickup, many of them with gunracks in the back windows. They looked at each other and shrugged. It was the story they were pursuing that was creepy, not a passing pickup.

Chapter 3

The Huntsville Motel, on the old road paralleling Route 45 a few miles short of the Huntsville town limits, sprawled conveniently opposite an exit ramp of the interstate.

The motel was distinguished by damp green shag carpeting in rooms that smelled of mildew. Cigarette butts floated in the kidney-shaped pool in the central court, and rust speckled the wrought-iron chairs at poolside. Travelers didn't come to the Huntsville Motel for the resort ambience. They came to sleep cheap on their way down to Houston and Galveston, where they hoped to find the decent jobs and lives that had eluded them in Oklahoma City or Denver; or they came to have a place to regroup before visiting a father or son or brother or mother locked up in one of the prisons in the Huntsville area. Visitors rarely stayed more than one night—never more than a week—and complaints about the accommodations were rare.

The journalists' first day in East Texas started out overcast and gray. It was sprinkling when Bitsey emerged from one of the rooms on the second floor.

She put up the umbrella she was carrying and walked past a room in which the occupants were shouting obscenities at each other behind the closed door. She walked down the stairs and crossed toward the motel coffee shop.

The coffee shop was a landmark of Generic Nondescript, containing nothing of regional or local color to pinpoint it geographically. Bitsey entered and passed down the same rows of Naugahyde booths she had seen in Newark, Cincinnatti, and Bakersfield. Only the Astros, Rangers, and Cowboys buttons in the box by the cash register would tell a sharp-eyed alien where in America he had landed.

Bitsey saw Zack at a corner table, smoking and reading.

A hypersmiley teenaged waitress approached Bitsey as she crossed the room. "How are you this morning?" the teenaged waitress said. She was a girl at the high point of cuteness and hope in her life, before an early marriage, kids, and chronic cash deficit started her on the downward path.

Bitsey ignored her, taking a menu without comment from the stack she held, as though the girl were a serving android. She slid into the booth across from Zack, reading the title of the book in which he was absorbed: *Dialogical Exhaustion* by David Gale.

"Little early for that, isn't it?" Bitsey said.

Zack lifted his cigarette. "The waitress told me Austin actually has a law that prohibits smoking in restaurants until after two p.m," he said, and pointed toward the exit with his butt. "If you get in the car and start driving now, Huntsville is only—"

"I meant the book," Bitsey said.

"*Dialogical Exhaustion*, by David Gale," Zack said. "The guy's a genius."

Bitsey opened her menu. "What time is it?" she said.

"Nine fifteen," Zack said. "There are like ten prisons around here. Death row is in the Ellis Unit, but they're moving it to the Terrell Unit at the end of the year." He gestured toward the kitchen. "The waitress's boyfriend works there. But her last boyfriend worked in the Huntsville Unit. And the two before that in Walker." He dropped his voice in a mockingly confiding tone. "The Estelle Unit has the cutest guys. But, and I'm quoting, 'My butt's too big to get an Estelle guy'."

"Fascinating," Bitsey said, reading the menu. She was not impressed by his attempt at being a reporter.

"Ellis is fifteen minutes out of town," Zack said. "So we've got . . . 5½ hours to kill." Then he thought: Wrong choice of words?

"Never eat in a place where the menus have pictures of the food and the cutlery comes in sanitized bags," Bitsey said half to herself.

"Maybe we should drive to Austin, check out the crime scene," Zack said. "Could be some good stuff for our story."

"This isn't *our* story," Bitsey said. "It's not even a story—it's an interview. Most importantly for you to remember, it's *my* interview."

"Okay, what do I get to watch *you* do for the next five hours?" Zack said good-naturedly.

"Drive around," Bitsey said sourly. "Looking for a decent restaurant."

"You know, Bitsey," Zack said, "your reputation as Mike Wallace with PMS just doesn't do you justice."

"My reputation got us invited here," Bitsey said. "I play by the rules, even if my colleagues don't like it. It's called . . ." Distracted, she took a napkin and wiped food particles and what looked like drool from the table.

"Ambition?" Zack said.

"Objectivity," Bitsey said with a look.

They stared at each other. She tossed the napkin onto the empty next table.

Zack picked up his book and started to read.

An awkward pool of silence spread out between them. The teenaged waitress interrupted. "So, y'all know what you're having?"

"Coffee," Bitsey said. "Just coffee."

The waitress left.

Bitsey looked at Zack. "Don't push me, smart-ass," she said. She stared out at the gloomy weather. She wondered why she was being so hard on this kid. Maybe it was just the assignment—the upcoming interview. Was there something hinky about the whole thing? Or more to the point, was there anything good about it?

She knew of several newsmagazine careers that had been ruined by biting on the wrong story. One was the European correspondent who convinced his magazine to shell out big dollars for the Hitler diaries, positive they were authentic; they were fakes. Another was the bureau chief who got and published an exclusive interview with D. B. Cooper, the hijacker who parachuted out of an airliner over the Pacific Northwest with $200,000 ransom and got away. It turned out not to be Cooper but U. R. Duped instead.

Bitsey had an uneasy feeling about this Gale story, but she couldn't put her finger on it. There was a big chunk of change involved here. If the story blew up and the word got out—and the word would get out—she would be the next cautionary she'll-never-get-another-byline-in-this-town-again tale told over drinks at P. J. Clarke's in Midtown.

Chapter 4

The drizzle made the country road they were driving seem like a passage from *The Grapes of Wrath*. Most of the fields they passed were fallow or unplowed stubble or patchy bean fields laced with weeds. These were subsistence farms, not high-powered agribusinesses. Farmhouses without windbreaks sat peeled to the gray wood from the subtropical storms that blasted in off the Gulf and battered East Texas seasonally. The rental car passed in front of a not exactly mainstream church—a weathered, out-of-kilter one-story box with a listing flat-topped bell tower and a message board that read, TO HELL WITH YOU—YOU KNOW WHO YOU ARE.

"You know you're in the Bible Belt when there are more churches than Starbucks," Bitsey said. They passed a sign in front of a clapboard church school that said, THIS IS GOD'S COUNTRY. PLEASE DON'T DRIVE THROUGH IT LIKE HELL.

"When there are more *prisons* than Starbucks," Zack said. A massive prison loomed into view. Billows of razor wire crowned the high walls.

Bitsey slowed the rental car as they came up on

the Texas flag sagging in the rain near the main gate. A brass plaque identified the complex as Ellis Unit. It was one of the maximum security branches of the Huntsville system and the one that housed death row. The condemned of Texas lived on death row, waiting to die soon, if their dates had been set, or waiting to die later, if their appeals were still running.

Bitsey and Zack cruised past. It was eerily quiet. Bitsey pulled to a stop by a corner guard tower with a sign that said, ALL VISITORS STOP HERE. They looked around.

"Now what?" Zack said.

"Get out and ask," Bitsey said. "You're the intern, remember?"

Zack wasn't sure he liked this idea. He got out of the car and looked up at the tower. A female guard talking on a cell phone at the top ignored him.

"Excuse me!" Zack said.

She turned away, still talking into the phone.

"Excuse me!" Zack said louder.

The female guard poked her head out of the tower.

"Hi," Zack said. "We're . . . we're from *NEWS Magazine*. We have an interview."

The guard gave him a bored look and turned back inside. She must have hit a button, because someone stirred inside the outdoor security kiosk by the main gate. A window slid open with a bang loud enough to draw Zack's attention. Bitsey and Zack walked down to it and presented themselves at the one-man security station—the prison's first line of defense against any bozos fixing to break in.

The two New Yorkers obeyed the speakered instructions to produce drivers' licenses. They slid them into a small tray that came out of the booth. A large hand scooped them up. The broad, leathery-visaged guard scrutinized their IDs with droopy, cynical eyes. He looked up at the man and woman to compare the likenesses. The applicants waited in the drizzle, Bitsey with an umbrella, Zack getting wet.

The entry gangway to Ellis Unit—between the gate and the main building—was a narrow run flanked by high fences and razor wire. An older guard silently led Bitsey and Zack from one salle-porte gate to the next. They passed into an empty foyer and the guard led the way through a side door into a reception office in the interior of Ellis Unit.

This was Duke Grover's front office. The prison flack was on the phone behind a counter as Bitsey and Zack entered. He waved them in and held up a just-a-sec finger.

"Ma'am, I am not gonna debate with you the rights and wrongs of this situation," Grover said into the phone. "Our job is to run a state prison system. . . ." He listened patiently. "Ma'am, this is not France. This is not Germany. This is Texas and we're gonna follow Texas law." He spoke with settled conviction: Them're the facts, like it or lump it. "You're very welcome, ma'am," he said. "Goodbye, now."

The office had wood paneling and a tired gray carpet. A portrait of Governor Bob Hardin—taken when he was a boyish fifty-something with slick, dyed-black hair—hung on one wall. A large aerial photograph of Ellis Unit hung on the opposite wall.

Grover hung up the phone. "Thank you, Margie," Grover said to a large, neighborly-looking woman who sat at a desk looking official. "Correspondents Bloom and Stevens, I presume," he said, turning to Bitsey and Zack with his patented cheesy smile.

"Yes, hello," Bitsey said.

They shook hands.

"Stemmons," Zack said.

"Stemmons," Grover said. "Sorry, it won't happen again. I'm Duke Grover, TDCJ Community Relations."

"He's usually real good with names," Margie said. The "real" had its own drawn-out Texas emphasis.

"And these days I always like to ask, now," Grover said unctuously to Bitsey, "do you prefer Miss, Mrs., or Ms.?"

"Bitsey," Bitsey said flatly, the hair on her neck prickling from the smug, Southern condescension oozing from this toad's fat lips. Texas-style good-ole-boy *courtoisie* was her surefire vomit inducer.

"Bitsey it is. Margie, I'm stealin' your umbrella," Grover said with a wink.

Margie gave him her oh-Grover-you-are-a-stitch wave. "Okey-dokey," she said with a grin.

Grover held the door while Bitsey and Zack filed past him out of the reception office.

"Bitsey, you ever been in a prison?" Grover said as they made their way along a gray-painted, concrete-floored corridor toward a barred section of the institution.

"Yes," Bitsey said.

"On death row?" Grover said.

"No," Bitsey said.

Zack smiled to himself. He was getting a fast firsthand dose of the Bitsey Bloom no-nonsense, no-wasted-words, professional reporter's style.

"All executions in the state of Texas occur over at

our Huntsville Unit downtown," Grover said. "But death row is here for the time being. This is home to all 442 offenders prior to their date. Average stay on the row is nine years. It'll put you off your supper, but then, it's supposed to." He gave a practiced smile: Death House humor. He had a barrel of 'em.

They came through to a key desk manned by a pretty, cool-eyed woman whose name tag read, CARLA MALAGOLI, and behind her a walk-through metal detector manned by a guard identified as JOE VITTI.

Joe was athletic, and he bounced slightly on the balls of his feet to show it.

"Joe . . . Carla," Grover said. "New York guests for Mr. Gale." He turned to the visitors. "IDs again, please," he said, adding brightly to Bitsey, "We've got three concerns here: safety, safety, and safety."

Bitsey kept an impassive face, but Zack could see her trying not to roll her eyes and kick this guy in the balls. She and Zack handed over their IDs to Carla, who vetted them and handed back red plastic badges saying, D.R. VISITOR.

"If you'd like to pin those on, please," Grover said. "The visitation area is entirely secure. We just ask you don't touch the glass. Windex gets expensive. You're not carryin' a weapon, are you, Bitsey?"

She didn't answer because she was looking past the metal detector down a hall leading to the main prison area, where a complex matrix of scary men and cold steel waited. She wasn't afraid—strange men in pickups at rest areas frightened her but not strange men locked behind iron bars. It was the oppressive feeling emanating from the dimly lit place the deeper they got into it that was affecting her.

"Bitsey?" Grover said.

"Sorry," Bitsey said. "No."

"Mr. Stemmons, you packin'?" Grover said.

"No, sir," Zack said.

"Cell phone?" Grover said.

"They're not working," Zack said. "No signal."

"Then you won't mind leavin' them here," Grover said.

Bitsey and Zack handed over their phones.

"We also have rules against the carrying of large sums of money and the wearing of open-toed shoes," Grover said. He looked at Bitsey's shoes.

She held up a foot. She was wearing low-heeled pumps with closed toes.

"Those will do just fine," Grover said. "Go on and walk through there, Bitsey." He motioned to the metal detector.

She walked through it.

"Open-toed shoes?" Zack said, showing himself to be a natural reporter. Even if you think you know why, ask anyway, Bitsey had said to him at one point. You'll almost always be surprised.

"Drives them crazy," Grover said. "Your turn, Mr. Stemmons."

Zack walked through. He *was* surprised by the answer, and chilled. He got a sudden picture of a world so desolate that the sight of a woman's foot in an open-toed shoe was dangerously stimulating. He went flat sober.

Grover followed. But he didn't lead them toward the main prison area. Instead he took a hard left down a side corridor flanking the permanent lockdown blocks.

"Now, should any kind of unpleasantness occur in

the visitation area," Grover said, "we ask that you stay put. And please follow the instructions of our fine correctional officers should they see fit to give you any."

To their right was a large picture window onto the prison barber shop. Three chairs were occupied by white-bibbed inmates getting haircuts from trustees holding scissors on safety wires. Seven other inmates waited their turns in molded plastic chairs bolted to the floor.

As Bitsey and Zack passed, every single man looked up and watched with a kind of spooky dead-pan intensity.

"Anythin' you say can be overheard," Grover said. "And any discussion of criminal activity on your part is admissible. Not plannin' a jailbreak, are you, Bitsey?"

Oh, you comedian, thought Bitsey, studying his flaccid neck and wishing she had a weapon.

Grover took another left out the door onto an open courtyard officially called the visitor's garden.

The three of them walked into an enclosed concrete square with a faux pond, a Japanese bridge, and some Astroturf—decorative elements straight from Home Depot. Though the yard was no more than thirty feet across, Grover popped his umbrella for Bitsey.

"This is our Japanese garden," Grover said. "We ask you not to throw coins in the pond."

Bitsey and Zack exchanged a look as Grover marched them somewhat proudly over the bridge. The setting, the decor, the insistently dorky PR man—for an instant it had an Alice in Wonderland air to it, which quickly dissipated as they entered a heavy mesh-windowed door on the other side.

"Here we are," Grover said.

The visitation hall was not what Bitsey had expected. She'd been in the visiting area of other prisons—noisy, hyperpopulated spaces filled with wives and kids and girlfriends and boyfriends all having a few laughs or an emotional moment or a bit of quiet communion with their caged relative or friend.

The physical feel here was the same—the yellowing linoleum and Pine-Sol ambience of an inner-city school cafeteria. But this room was quiet. They were the sole visitors. Things were different on death row.

In the center island, the visitation cubicles, with two long rows of mini-cages backing them, were empty. At the back of the room sat a supervising guard on a raised dais. He was no Andy Griffith. He was a lean side of beef and he looked like he meant business. A similarly alert and dour door guard sat inside the prisoners' island. A third patrolling guard moved conspicuously around the visitors' area.

On the visitors' side, hard, straight-backed chairs were lined up along the window counters as though for unemployment benefits counseling. Getting up from a chair in the hall's center, a big man wearing a baggy suit and black cowboy boots turned toward them. He gave them a half smile.

This was David's lawyer, Braxton Belyeu.

On the prisoners' side, in one of the metal cages, sat David Gale.

Chapter 5

"All yours, Mr. Belyeu," Grover said with a short salute for the lawyer. He gave his cheesy official's smile to Bitsey and Zack. "You folks have a safe visit now," he said as he moved toward the door.

"Thank you," Bitsey said, looking around, scoping the place out. Her reporter's eye was at work, looking for the few killer details that would make the scene come alive in an introduction to the interview she would eventually file to the magazine.

Grover exited. Bitsey and Zack made their way toward Belyeu and Gale.

"Miss Bloom?" Belyeu said. When he spoke, his accent was Louisiana Cajun via Harvard Yard.

"Yes," Bitsey said.

"Did that PR man validate your parkin'?" Belyeu said.

"He said the gift shop could do it," Bitsey said.

Belyeu laughed. "She's a smart one," he said to Gale.

Belyeu took a few steps forward and extended his hand. "Braxton Belyeu, Mr. Gale's attorney," he said.

"This is Zack," Bitsey said.

"Pleasure," Belyeu said.

"And this is the man of the hour," Belyeu said, turning toward Gale.

Another Southern charmer, thought Bitsey, at the same time pondering the strange note on which he introduced the condemned man—darkly comic and ironic.

Gale politely stood up, but he was too tall for his cage and he had to hunch over. He smiled.

As the three civilians moved toward him, a sudden blare from the loudspeaker startled them. "Sit down, Gale," barked the overamplified voice of the supervising guard. "Prisoner will not stand."

All except Gale flinched at this harsh intrusion— which served its purpose: to remind all that this was no tea room, this was no cocktail lounge, abide by the tight rules or the party's over.

Gale sat and smiled again, a bit embarrassed. He was still a strikingly handsome man, though pallid of face and thinned down by prison food. He had several days' growth of beard and he wore the standard white prison jumpsuit. His steady dark-eyed gaze bespoke an undimmed intelligence and a continuing interest in the world around him.

"Hello," Gale said.

"Hello," Bitsey said neutrally, eyeballing this convicted killer, searching his demeanor for hints of character, motives.

"Hi," Zack said.

"Now, why can't they turn that thing down?" Belyeu said, looking around at the seated supervising guard.

"My lawyer respectfully suggests you adjust the

speaker system volume," Gale said, looking across at the guard.

They waited. They all looked over at the supervising guard on the raised platform. A mike on an articulated arm protruded from the wall. The guard, without changing expression, made a get-on-with-your-business gesture.

Bitsey sat down in the chair next to Belyeu. Zack hovered behind her.

"They're practicing being cruel and unusual," Gale said.

"Miss Bloom, I'm sure you're a-bitin' at the bit," Belyeu said. The lawyer collected papers from the chair he was using and started to stuff them into his well-worn leather bag. "Now, it is our understanding that you are to have three two-hour sessions," Belyeu said. "Today, tomorrow, and Thursday, all at three in the p.m. I'm sorry we can't afford you more time, but contrary to popular rumor we have not yet begun to fight. It is our understanding that you will do this alone."

"The magazine would prefer if I . . ." Zack said.

"Alone," Bitsey said with finality. "Understood."

Zack shot her a look. She did not bother to return it, keeping her eyes on Gale.

"Fine," Belyeu said. "It's also our understanding that you will do this with no recording equipment of any kind. Now, I have some paper for which I need your Jo Ann Hancock," Belyeu said pointedly, handing her a business card. "Come by my Austin office at your earliest convenience. Thursday mornin', say."

Bitsey was confused. This was a new requirement, not mentioned in the oft-repeated arrangements. She was wary. She didn't take kindly to being waltzed around.

Belyeu just smiled at her, then looked over at the patrolling guard. She finally understood that he was simply talking about the money and nodded.

"Fine, till Thursday then," Belyeu said. He picked up his bag. He motioned for Zack to precede him, and together they started the hike to the door. Belyeu turned and, walking backward, said, "Good luck, Miss Bloom." To Gale he said, "I'll come by later." He turned back toward the door. "Mr. Zack?" he said. "What say you and me partake of a death-defying cigarette in the visitors' car park? 'Bye, y'all," he called, as they exited.

More of that strange death row humor, Bitsey thought.

She turned her full attention to Gale. They were alone—but for the two guards. And face-to-face— with the glass between them, of course. Suddenly they were both uncomfortable.

"So . . ." Bitsey said.

"Pull up your seat," Gale said.

She moved her chair closer.

Gale smiled at her—he had a beautiful smile: sincere, charming, vaguely devilish.

"He's quite a character," Bitsey said, referring to Belyeu and deflecting that smile by looking down, starting to rummage through her purse looking for her reporter's notebook and pen. She knew exactly where the pad and pen were; it was a gambit she used to compose herself or ease through an awkward moment.

"Yeah, he's about the only outside contact I have left," Gale said. "And a good friend."

"Where's your ex-wife?" Bitsey said. She took the notepad out of her purse and affected searching for a pen.

"I don't want you to mention her, or my son," Gale said. "That's part of the deal."

"All right," Bitsey said. "Anything else, just clearly say, 'Off the record.' I'll take it to my grave. You can trust me on that." She held up a pen. "Does this count as recording equipment?"

He shrugged. "How do we start?" he said.

"We start with you telling me what I'm doing here," the reporter said.

Gale looked at her for a moment. "No one who looks through that glass sees a person. They see a crime," he said. "I'm not David Gale. I'm a murderer and a rapist four days short of his execution. You're here because I want to be remembered as much for how I led my life as how it ended."

She considered him a moment, then scribbled that rather pat, uninformative, and disingenuous-sounding declaration in her notebook. Wasn't she really here as a last desperate attempt to save this guy's ass? His talking about how his life ended made him sound like a man way past denial, a man accepting a grim fate. She expected a man grasping at the straw that a national newsmagazine story might represent.

"Why me?" Bitsey said.

"I know you're good," Gale said. "Your colleagues' respect for you isn't tainted by affection."

She gave him a look. That was good. That one was in there for an ace, delivered like a pro.

He gave her a neutral smile.

"Tell me your story, Mr. Gale," Bitsey said. She

had a grudging respect for a man who could so succinctly zing her, compliment her, and offer an explanation all at the same time.

"Six years ago . . ." Gale started in. No preamble. Cut to the chase.

Chapter 6

On a bitter cold late afternoon six years prior, snow flurries swirled around the institution that locals called "the Walls." The Texas Department of Corrections Prison, Huntsville Unit. The famous Huntsville prison. Actually, several prison compounds—clustered a few miles apart, gathered in one location for practicality's sake—fell under that general name. Immense redbrick ramparts with corner guard towers occupied an entire city block. It dominated the little town. The entrance to the prison resembled the gateway to a nineteenth-century textile factory in Industrial Revolution England. Crowning the brick facade was a gabled clock. It now read 6:18.

Across the street was the prison's administration building and, with it, Welcome House, an ironic name for a structure on the grounds of an institution of penal and retributive intent. Its purpose wasn't to welcome new miscreants, of course, but their visitors, as well as occasional dignitaries and the media, when the need arose. Half of Welcome House's yard had been roped off on this occasion to form a large press area. It dwarfed the present media contingent—

three bored photographers who hugged themselves against the cold and kept an eye on the prison's glass doors.

Down the street, a crowd-control roadblock kept back just two onlookers. A fundamentalist justice seeker held a sign—AN EYE FOR AN EYE!—and periodically called out his Hammurabic imprecation.

Beside him stood a cowboy in typical urban Western wear: the forward-tilting Stetson, boots, denims, ranch jacket. He waved no sign or placard, but held a cell phone to his ear. He hummed the melody of a Puccini aria and checked his pocket watch against the gabled clock across the street. Impenetrable dark eyes in a lean, lined face gave no hint which side he was on.

The watch's minute hand changed from 6:18 to 6:19.

A hundred thirty-five miles cross-country to the west in the state capital, a dingy wall clock in a set of makeshift offices read 6:19.

The low-budget setup looked like a storefront campaign headquarters for a local political race—tight and narrow, no frills, no glitz or glamour. A cluster of beat-up gray metal desks held the tools of the trade: computers and multiline telephones, Xerox machines, hand-printed posters, stacks of flyers and envelopes, and a stamp machine.

Beneath the clock a simple banner identified the place as DEATHWATCH AUSTIN.

One wall was lined with neat rows of black-and-white photographs, head shots, mostly men, nearly three dozen in all.

The people pictured on the wall were death row

inmates. About one in every three had diagonal red-marker crosses over their faces.

"It's probably been about seven minutes," Josh said.

Five people sat in cold silence—activists in waiting. They were the core members of this abolish-the-death-penalty group, whose latest cause hung in the balance, as it were, at Huntsville.

Josh, a skinny college kid with a mullet haircut and a pinch of Skoal in his cheek, stared at a computer screen. The University of Texas–Austin was a magnet for idealistic liberal-minded youth, and Josh had found a comfortable home there. The sprawling, city-sized campus was an island of open-minded, progressive thought in the middle of an unwaveringly conservative part of the country. Social causes were a large part of the undergraduate experience. Josh had invested in his cause. He worked through a programming problem to ease his agitated mind.

Beth, too, had found her cause. She had come to U.T.–Austin from a well-heeled home in the affluent Oaks section of Houston. Both her parents were physicians, and both worked in inner-city hospitals as trauma doctors who spent their days patching up lives dealt with cheaply or heedlessly. They had passed on to their daughter a reverence for life of all kinds and a need to commit to its preservation. Beth sat hunched at her desk, coddling a Styrofoam cup of coffee, sobbing quietly.

Rosie, a competent, matronly woman, was a volunteer of a different cut. She came to DeathWatch by way of the U.S. Navy, where she had been a lifer. On board a ship hit by a terrorist bomb in the Mediterranean, she had witnessed carnage firsthand—her fellow sailors mutilated and dying gruesomely as she crouched over them spattered with their blood. It had left her unreconciled to human killing in any form and ended her romance with the institutions of war, no matter how patriotic. She had resigned and found a new career as an administrator at an occupational school in downtown Austin. Joining DeathWatch was her way of opposing killing on the home front, the state-sponsored kind. She sat at a desk holding a phone to one ear and watching the clock.

Constance Harraway—slim, attractive, in her mid-thirties—grew up with no inkling she would one day be sitting vigil on the fate of murderers and rapists with whom she'd had no previous earthly connection. She was a woman with a profession, a Ph.D-credentialed associate professor of philosophy at U.T. She was a step away from tenure and assured of earning it, barring some sort of neutron bomb exploding in her life or career. Her student evaluations were consistently high, she published regularly in scholarly journals, and she was held in high esteem by her colleagues as one who never shirked duty on the various onerous committees that burden academics.

Beside her sat David Gale, a lean, dark-eyed man also in his mid-thirties whose intense gaze radiated both humor and serious intelligence. Gale now stared down morosely at the lettering on his blue Yale sweatshirt and picked at it with barely restrained fury.

Dr. Gale was a somebody in his field, a full philosophy professor, a deep thinker and writer with a national reputation who nevertheless would run away screaming rather than be called Doctor.

This evening he was powerless; he felt like a nobody. The great truths of his immense learning churned in his brain in twisted and bastardized form: "The powerless life is not worth living" . . . "Clout is all we apparently know on earth and all we need to know" . . . "I think, therefore I am not worth a bucket of warm spit. . . ."

Inside the Huntsville Unit of the Texas Department of Corrections—the Death House—the end was approaching for one man. José Maria Velasco, former farmworker, drug smuggler, drunken multiple killer. Wild fear sloshed in his gut and panic poured from his eyes. He was in restraints on the gurney, his arms wide spread, strapped to boards and rigged with IVs. He was watching the clock on the wall, now a few minutes past six p.m., as it squeezed his remaining time on earth toward nothing.

Velasco had arrived at the unit twelve hours earlier, already in full dread, breathing in short, quick bursts, his hands shaking. Fear of what he expected to be stabbing, paralyzing, agonizing final moments had seized his heart sometime in the twenty-four hours before his transfer from death row at Ellis Unit and gradually tightened his chest until he could no longer take a full breath.

The prisoner had then had some respite—thanks to the calming influence of the prison chaplain, who was there waiting for him when he arrived. The veteran of nearly a hundred executions at Huntsville Unit, the Presbyterian chaplain was practiced at easing the worst pain of inmates' last hours. He had done thirty-five this year alone.

He assured the man, or more rarely the woman, that he would not die in pain or alone—that the lethal injection procedure was painless, and that he, the chaplain, would go with the prisoner into the death chamber and stay with him to the end. The chaplain explained the drill of the next few hours— short visits from family or spiritual adviser; talk or silence as the prisoner chose; writing letters and final phone calls; rehearse his last words, if he wanted to say any; shower and change into civilian clothes; last meal; and execution itself. When the hour came, the chaplain would say only, "It's time to go." And they would walk the five paces to the heavy metal door and pass into the execution chamber.

Now, trussed in crucifixion position in the death chamber, José Maria Velasco thought the idea of making peace was insane. In no direction lay comfort for this scared soul, not even in the kind chaplain standing with his hand on the man's ankle. Velasco's heinous deeds had wrought an unspeakable end. The clammy darkness was about to wrap around him and suffocate him; the light was about to go out forever. Now, in the last few minutes before the chemicals flowed into his veins and seized his heart, he was near mad with terror.

At DeathWatch, Constance stared at nothing while biting her lip. She was stunned with a sudden weariness.

David Gale closed his eyes and fought to calm his thrumming pulse.

They both knew exactly what was going on at Huntsville; they knew the particulars of readying a man for death and the now-practiced routine of state killing. They knew all the gruesome details of death-by-government in the name of justice and vengeance, and they thought it was wrong. They agreed with the logic of the question nearly every death row inmate asked in his final hours: How can the state kill a person to show others that killing is wrong?

The wall clock read 6:19. They watched the minute hand change from 6:19 to 6:20.

At the Huntsville Unit, a man emerged through the glass double doors into the icy evening air. Duke Grover, the prison public relations officer, was making his entrance, followed by five others.

One of the photographers bestirred himself. "Grover's comin' out," he said. He raised his camera and flipped off the lens cap.

"Six twenty," the second photographer said, taking a photo of the clock.

The third photographer murmured a rap refrain as he photographed Grover leading five tense civilians down the stairs. From the look on his face, the head flack could have been escorting celebrities to their seats at the Oscars.

A fleshy-faced career bureaucrat with a comb-over, a narrow tie, and a we-aim-to-please smile, Grover made no apologies for what they did there at the unit. He had willingly bought into the capital punishment revival that came to Texas in 1982, after a ten-year moratorium. The U.S. Supreme Court had deemed executions "inhumane" in 1972 and had effectively outlawed capital punishment. The Texas legislature revised the Texas Penal Code to get around that prohibition, and Grover was at his post when Charles Brooks, Jr., was the first to be killed by the new, "humane" method—lethal injection. Grover would give special visitors a Death House tour that included a glimpse of "Old Sparky," the oak electric chair that, with its own generator as power source, had fried 361 Texas prison inmates over the years.

Grover felt it was his—*their*—job to carry out the will of the people and they did it well. He did not shy away from these occasions to meet the press; it was his chance to put the Department's best face out there—in his humble estimation, his own.

"They're bringin' his witnesses out," the urban Cowboy down the street behind the crowd-control barricade said into his cell phone.

The eye-for-an-eye pro-death cheerleader let out a whoop and waved his placard, hoping to get his picture in the paper. None of the photographers bit.

In Austin, DeathWatch volunteer Josh registered something on his computer screen. "Okay, we got an official pronouncement at . . . six twenty," Josh said. He recorded the time. "Number thirty-six this year for the Great State of Texas."

They all exchanged looks: They'd lost. Again.

David took in a long breath and stood.

"David, don't start throwing things," Constance said.

"I need to get home," David said. "Let's do the press release tomorrow."

Another phone rang. Constance reached for it. It had to be a media call. "Go. I'll do it," she said.

He nodded and walked mechanically toward the door.

It was one of the main reasons Welcome House had been built at Huntsville Unit: to accommodate the lively media interest in the capital punishment renewal. Texans were foursquare in favor of it, this tough-minded official action designed to protect and deter. If it was rough justice, the law of the Old West, so much the better.

Grover escorted the five witnesses to a podium in front of Welcome House, where the three photographers each snapped off a roll of obligatory photos. A dark-haired, plainly dressed woman with a perm—one of the murder victims' mothers—stepped to the rostrum. She pulled a well-worn piece of paper from her purse and stared at it for a beat, as though recognizing, at this much anticipated payoff moment, its pitiful inadequacy.

Her face and voice suggesting years of smoking and none-too-easy living, she read: "Today we got justice. We have waited eleven long years for this day." She spoke expressionlessly, more worn-out and joyless than grieving. "I wish my daughter could have had eleven more birthdays. . . ."

The photographers started to put their cameras away. They'd got their shot; the job was over.

The woman stopped as she and the other four witnesses watched the three photographers turn and walk away, talking among themselves. Pulling herself up, the mother continued her prepared speech to no one. "Eleven more birthdays and eleven more Christmases," she said. "I wish I'd've seen her graduate from high school this year with all her classmates. I wish . . ."

In the DeathWatch office, Constance walked to the wall of photos. With a Magic Marker she marked a red X over the black-and-white head shot of a Hispanic male. José Maria Velasco joined the list of human X-outs, a rapidly growing list in the State of

Texas. The Lone Star State claimed nearly three hundred of the eight-hundred-plus kills carried out in the U.S. since reinstatement. It was by far the champion execution state, with states like Virginia and Florida vying for a distant second at under a hundred each.

Rosie turned away, busying herself straightening the tables, throwing now-pointless flyers and mailings in a large trash bin. Josh and Beth compared calendars, conferring about the timing for the next case, wondering if the plan of action should be the same, or if they could somehow do more the next time, or different.

Exiting the office, David made his way listlessly toward his twelve-year-old Volvo station wagon parked down the street. Behind him, the DeathWatch headquarters sat indistinguishable among a row of abandoned storefronts.

He collapsed into the driver's seat and put his head back tiredly. Another day, another flop. He grabbed a bottle of Black Bush Irish whiskey from the glove compartment and poured three good inches into a travel cup. He started the car and pulled away from the curb.

He rolled through the seedy, semi-industrial area south of downtown, heading toward College Park. He turned onto an avenue and stopped at a red light, taking a stiff hit from his travel cup. A highway patrol car pulled up on his right. The patrolman in the black-and-tan gave David a cursory glance.

David stared at the patrolman, who looked neutrally ahead. Behind his head, the policeman's seatbelt buckle caught the light.

David rolled down his passenger-side window. "Hey!" he said.

The patrolman ignored him.

"Hey! Officer!" David said.

The patrolman looked over. He rolled down his window, expecting a confrontation. David pointed to the seat-belt buckle.

"Your seat belt," David said.

The patrolman nodded—mildly embarrassed, annoyed. He reached back for the belt and buckled himself in. He keyed his window back up without looking again at David and, when the light changed, drove on.

David raised his glass to the departing officer, drank to his health and to the foreshortened life of José Maria Velasco. And then drank again to the futility of his puny efforts to bring this eye-for-an-eye state into the civilized twenty-first century. He drove on.

Chapter 7

The University of Texas in Austin is a good-sized city within a city: fifty thousand students; close to ten thousand faculty and staff; its own police force and fire department to oversee a vast, 357-acre campus; its own governance; and definitely its own socio-political identity. Texas is a conservative state. You want liberal, go to the Ivy League or to one of the other effete Eastern institutions; go to the U. of Wisconsin, go to Berkeley.

Or . . . stay home and go to U.T.–Austin.

It is a strangely progressive, live-and-let-live, left-leaning enclave in the heart of the conservative South. It is a testament to American tolerance and diversity that even the most chauvinistic Texans will look with pride on this redheaded stepchild in their midst and call it their own. It makes every bit of sense that the "Outlaw" Texas C&W music of Willie and Waylon and Jerry Jeff Walker sprang from the fertile ground of populist, ornery, unpretentious Austin.

On a sunny day in spring, a female philosophy grad student named Berlin hurried across the leafy campus. Wide-set green eyes, casually flying auburn hair, unself-consciously sexy ways of moving—Berlin was God's gift to college boys and quite aware of it. If her brains and work habits matched her sultry physical gifts, she was a young woman who was going somewhere.

If, however, she was as late habitually as she was on this particular day—checking her watch, breaking into a run—her future was not so assured.

In U.T. Lecture Hall 109 in the Blackwell Philosophy and Religion Center, a mixture of graduate and undergraduate students sat attuned to every word of popular lecturer Professor David Gale. They were laughing, edified and entertained, as Gale, from a mike at the podium, dryly skewered some of the sacred cows of modern European, post-Derrida, semiotic phenomenology before moving on to one of his favored modern thinkers, Lacan.

Thirty attentive students—the maximum number he allowed in the always oversubscribed class—listened appreciatively as he lectured. A young, smooth-faced thirty-four, full of physical and intellectual vitality, David looked like a grad student himself. On the whiteboard behind him he had scrawled phrases: *Lacan*, *objet petit a*, and *Fantasy Theory*.

"Think," David said. "What do you fantasize about? World peace?" No one responded. "Thought so."

Light laughter from the students.

"Do you fantasize about international fame?"

Some of the guys applauded; others then booed them.

"Do you fantasize about winning a Pulitzer? A Nobel? An MTV Music Award?"

Some hearty applause.

"Do you fantasize about some genius hunk—ostensibly bad but secretly simmering with noble passions, and willing to sleep on the wet spot?"

The women laughed and applauded. "I'll take two!" a large female grad student called out. She got a big laugh.

The whole class was engaged. David had them on his wavelength, building skillfully toward his main point. "Do you fantasize about meeting a Victoria's Secret model," David said, "just slumming between law school and running her family's Vastly Endowed Foundation for Tragically Sad-Eyed Children?"

Again the crowd laughed, and David abruptly changed tone.

"Okay, good, you see Lacan's point," he said. "Fantasies *must* be unrealistic. The minute you get something, you don't, *you can't*, want it anymore. To continue to exist, desire needs objects to be perpetually absent. So desire supports itself with crazy fantasies. . . ."

Berlin, the eminently desirable grad student, entered loudly from a side door, out of breath and discombobulated, looking for all the world like a *Playboy*-goes-Texas-co-ed fold-out. The crowd howled at the timing.

David paused, letting the moment play out.

"Sorry," Berlin said, frozen to the spot.

David animatedly gestured toward the seats. He waited several moments as she crossed and slid into one.

"This is what Pascal means," he went on, "when he says the only time we're truly happy is when daydreaming about future happiness."

Berlin adjusted herself and her books.

"Or why we say, 'The hunt is sweeter than the

kill,' or 'Be careful what you wish for,' " David said.
"Some anthropologists claim that the only aphorism
that exists in every culture is some version of 'The
grass is always greener on the other side of the
fence.' "

Berlin's roommate, an equally glamorous if more
punctual student, had saved her a seat on the aisle.
She handed Berlin a sealed letter marked REGISTRAR'S
OFFICE and whispered, "It came today."

Berlin considered the envelope, turning it over
with a dubious look—but didn't open it.

"Not because you'll get it, but because you're
doomed not to want it if you do," David said. "You
can't want what you already have. Think about it
next time you're at a wedding."

More laughter, equally from the guys and the girls.

Berlin nervously shoved the unopened registrar's
letter into a book.

As the hour ended and the students poured out
the double doors leading from David's class, they
passed a woman about David's age waiting in the
crowded hallway.

Standing against the wall, studying a document
she'd pulled from a file under her arm, was Constance Harraway—Associate Professor Harraway.
Constance wore glasses and granola clothes—the
earth shoes and rope-belted sack dress sort of garb
popular with the humanities crowd in universities.

In the lecture hall, as the students were filing out,
David turned from the whiteboard and gathered his
papers at the podium. Berlin approached him.

"Sorry about being late," she said with a rueful
but winning smile. "There was, you know, a thing."

"There usually is, Berlin," David said.

"Look, I know I'm not doing well," Berlin said.

David nodded, taking his books and papers off the podium.

"And to torture a cliché," the girl said, "I'd do anything to pass."

He looked at her for a beat, then started to walk toward the door.

"Anything, Professor Gale," she said with a sweet, pleading voice.

He stopped, turned. Considered. "Anything, huh?" he said.

"*Any*thing," Berlin said suggestively. She put on a solicitous, charming smile.

David checked the room to make sure they were alone, then went over to her, leaning down close to her face.

"Tell you what," he said quietly. "I'll give you a good grade, a really good grade, if you will"—he leaned in closer to her ear and whispered sensually—"study."

He smiled, turned, and walked away. As she watched him go out the double doors, her face flushed and anger flared in her eyes.

As David emerged into the hallway, Constance looked up and hurried over to join him. She was excited. She spoke—as she invariably did—with absolute conviction and authority. They talked as they walked down the crowded hall.

"Hey," David said.

"The T.A. finished transcribing all the governor's radio and TV commercials," Constance said. "Listen to this gem. Journalist: 'Governor, don't you think three executions a week is excessive?' Governor: 'I say, bring 'em in, strap 'em down, and let's rock and roll.' "

"It's good to know our governor is in touch with his inner frat boy," David said.

She handed him a copy of the transcriptions.

"Tell me again why *you* aren't doing the debate?" David said, as they emerged into the sunshine outside the lecture hall.

"Telegenics," Constance said. "You have a cuter butt."

"I hadn't noticed," David said.

"I know," Constance said.

"That's not what I meant," David said.

They walked catty-corner across the tree-lined mall. The campus and its famous tower rose up the hill behind them.

"He'll do the whole down-home wisdom thing," Constance said. " 'Capital punishment is God's law. An eye for an eye,' and all that. Stick to rational arguments about facts."

They came to a sidewalk junction and stopped. Students passed them in a hurry to make their next classes. Every few seconds a student or faculty member would call out a "Hey, Professor" to David or Constance as they passed.

"And watch your ego," Constance said. "Don't come across as one of those I-hate-authority-because-everyone-round-here-wears-big-hats-and-nobody-in-charge-reads-the–*New Yorker* types."

"Anything else?" David said.

"I'm getting new federal stats from Amnesty tonight," Constance said.

"Bring them to Greer's party," David said.

She looked at him earnestly over the top of her glasses.

"I have papers to grade, and if you have a hangover tomorrow . . ."

"I'm walking away now," David said, hands up, moving away.

"Ten o'clock!" Constance said, calling after him. Silence. "Bright-eyed and bushy-tailed!" she called.

"Bushy-tailed," David said, looking back with his famous crooked smile. He waved.

Chapter 8

The Gale family lived in as posh and shady a part of town as the University itself. Stately homes sat back from a street lined with giant, overhanging oaks. The Gale place was a semirestored two-story white clapboard-and-brick town house far grander than most university professors could afford. The front lawn was lush, manicured, and bracketed with carefully trimmed shrubs. A long rope swing hung from a giant, ancient silver maple in the backyard. David's Volvo sat in the broad driveway in front of the two-car garage beside his wife's much newer, hipper Jeep. A new red VW Beetle sat parked to one side.

David turned off the light in the bathroom adjacent to his son's bedroom on the second floor and came in holding Jamie's jeans and shoes. On the dad's T-shirt it said, EVIL-DOER & CURIOUS PERSON. Jamie, an irresistible six-year-old with his father's intense dark eyes, sat in bed holding a stuffed sheep in the air.

"Jamie," David said. "Did you mark your calendar?"

"Yep," Jamie said, looking up at it on the wall opposite the bed.

Jamie's calendar counted the days until his mother's return. He had ten frowny faces over ten consecutive days, then four empty days, and then a large smiley face day. The frowny faces were in a kid's hand, the smiley face in an adult's.

"Only . . . four more days till Mommy comes home," Jamie said, counting.

David put away the jeans and shoes in the closet, which was surprisingly neat and well organized.

"Only four," David said. "That's great, huh?"

"Can I ask something?" Jamie said. "It's really, really, really important."

"Sure," David said, concerned.

"Can we have pancakes for breakfast?" Jamie said.

David laughed and came over to the bed. "Okay," he said.

"With syrup and strawberries," Jamie said with a big grin.

"We'll see," David said.

"And chocolate shavers," Jamie said.

"Chocolate shav*ings*," David said.

"And whipped cream," Jamie said, beaming.

"Whipped cream," David said, tucking him in. "Go to sleep." He kissed the boy. "Good night, Jamie."

"Do Cloud Dog too," Jamie said, holding up his stuffed sheep.

"Good night, Cloud Dog," David said, kissing the stuffed sheep.

Jamie smiled in satisfaction and closed his eyes. David moved to the door, turning for a last look at his son before pulling the door to behind him.

The living room of the Gale home was Bohemian Cool. Framed black-and-white photographs of the march on Selma, and images by Lewis Hine and Jacob Riis sat comfortably with modern artworks. Saving the place from Martha Stewart pseudoelegance were piles and piles of books to add to the long, tall shelves of books.

A baby-sitter sat on the couch reading a school textbook, holding lip gloss, and absentmindedly applying it as she read. Next to her on the couch lay her Walkman from whose headphones came the faint strains of a Britney Spears CD.

David came down the stairs, grabbed his jacket from the railing, and passed her on his way across the living room. "Back before midnight," he said, heading out the front door.

"That's fine, Mr. Gale," the baby-sitter said. "Don't do anything I wouldn't," she called after him.

"Oh, I don't think there's any danger of that," David said as he disappeared into the night.

When she heard the door close, the baby-sitter reached for the TV remote.

Professor Greer lived in a house as grand in its own ways as Gale's, but unfortunately for Greer, it was not his for the keeping. Perched beside the Colorado River, which cut through the city garlanded by a cooling greenbelt of hiking and bike trails, it was a choice place to live—a rambling Victorian with pool deck and river access. It was one of the houses the university owned and made available to certain faculty chairs.

The large living room opened onto a patio and pool directly on the river. Packed inside and scattered around outside were forty or so invited party guests—mostly grad students with a liberal sprinkling of faculty—and a good quorum of uninvited campus party hounds. Many of the revelers wore T-shirts with philosophic/intellectual/artsy slogans: ESSENTIALIST, YAWNIC, MAD, BAD, AND DANGEROUS TO KNOW, DECONSTRUCT THIS!, THE CELIBATE LIFE IS NOT WORTH LIVING, LET THEM EAT CATEGORICAL IMPERATIVES. Leonard Cohen and Dar Williams music played simultaneously in different parts of the party.

From the front door Anson Greer, a Humpty-Dumptyesque middle-ager wearing a HOST T-shirt, escorted David into the living room. "The guy's the Immanuel Kant of the NFL," Greer said. "Consistent, accurate, effective, and boring, boring, boring."

David laughed, giving him no argument. They passed a slim, thoughtful-looking man wearing Walkman headphones and a T-shirt that said AD ASTRA PER JERRY GARCIA. They both chuckled.

Greer left David with John—a fat-faced linguistics professor in his sixties with a homemade T-shirt that said, PRE-SOCRATIC pulled over his shirt and tie—as well as with Ross, a late-forties English lit professor wearing his HOMOSEXUALIST T-shirt. Greer went on into the open kitchen.

"John," David said. "Ross."

"Hello, David," Ross said.

"Professor Gale," John said. "Where's your better half?"

"Better half?" David said. "Oh, wife. Spain. She's in Spain."

"Again?" John said. "I *am* sorry." He nodded and moved away, heading for the outdoor part of the party on the patio.

David watched him go, thinking: Forgive John. His first two wives left him and his third, whom he deserved, refused to.

Ross dragged him by the arm to the snacks display

on a large wooden counter between living room and kitchen. It was oh-so *Gourmet*. The counter was neatly laid with finger food and dips, and ranks of bottles of drinkables and mixer and glasses. The flower arrangement was perfect.

"Looks like my wife's affair is an open secret," David said, positioning himself opposite Ross across the counter as they began methodically to graze.

"Hermeneutical bias," Ross said. "The only fun truths are the ones someone's trying to hide."

"She's been to Barcelona four times in a year," David said with a kind of philosophical resignation. "I don't think she's trying to hide anything."

"Well, her father *is* the ambassador," Ross said.

"The embassy is in Madrid," David said.

An uncomfortable beat. They munched some finger food. Ross finally gestured for David to lean close over the counter. "By the way," he said low, "Berlin's here—and pretty livid. We've expelled her. She received the letter today, took the opportunity to throw a fit in my office. You should—"

"Talking about me?" Berlin said.

Her beautiful head suddenly popped in between them.

"Yep," David said. "As a matter of fact, we are."

She was tipsy. She leaned up and whispered in David's ear, "Did he tell you I said when you were circumcised they threw away the wrong part?" Berlin said.

"He mentioned it," David said.

She reached over and took Ross's drink from his hand, drank the rest, and gave it back.

"It's called schmuck," David said.

"What?" Berlin said.

"The part of the foreskin that gets thrown away," David said. "I think it's called schmuck."

"Aren't we so fucking clever," Berlin said. She leaned against the counter and looked him steadily in the eye. Her high-amp green eyes were capable of stirring up pulse rates across a room.

"I think perhaps I should get us another," Ross said, escaping. "David?"

"Black Bush," David said, watching Berlin, wary of her mood, warier of those green eyes.

Ross walked to the refrigerator. Berlin and David stood straight. Her midriff T-shirt read, I COME FIRST.

"You were a jerk this afternoon," Berlin said.

"For what it's worth, I didn't know about the expulsion," David said gently.

"Is that supposed to be an apology?" Berlin said.

"More like a conciliation," David said.

Ross placed two gin-and-tonics on the food counter and turned back to finish pouring David's Black Bush. He handed it to him, took his own drink, and moved away.

By midevening, Greer's living room was a free-for-all, and his patio had lost all of its early-party civilized charm. Midparty chaos reigned. The food counter was a trough of spilled food, empty bottles, flowers in disarray. Dance music thumped loudly from the CD changer as Berlin crossed to the booze table and took a bottle. A newcomer would be hard put to distinguish this high-level faculty party from an undergraduate Greek-weekend beer bust.

Berlin made her way with studied steadiness through the living room, where a few people now danced—not elegantly—and out onto the patio.

The number of revelers on the patio who were cer-
tifiably drunk had reached a critical mass, so the air
itself gave off a contagious vibe of let-it-rip licen-
tiousness. A crowd by the pool surrounded two patio
chairs that were pulled up facing each other. In one
David sat. His good friend Ross occupied the other.
The men were playing an Irish drinking game, and
the crowd, including Berlin, were choosing favorites
and rooting them on. And true to their lofty callings,
these combatants weren't satisfied to be playing any
crude party sex game like Truth or Dare, but were
matching wits, or at least half of them.

"All right," Ross said. He cleared his throat—he
was slurring a bit—and recited:

> As the poets have mournfully sung,
> Death takes the innocent young,
> The screamingly funny,
> The rolling in money,
> And those who are very well hung.

The well-lit crowd rewarded his offering with
laughter peppered with animated groans.

David raised his glass to Ross and downed an Irish
whiskey. Someone started to chant: "Gale! Gale!
Gale!"

David, feeling very much in control—something of
a delusion—intoned:

> There once was a lesbian from Canjuom,
> who took a young man to her room,
> and they argued all night,
> as to who had the right,
> to do what, how, and to whom.

He was rewarded with laughter, except from two thirty-something women who were holding each other. They decided a few boos were in order. Ross gave them a solemn nod, and drank his gin-and-tonic.

"One more," Berlin said. "C'mon, one more."

"Enough," David said. "That's enough."

The crowd wanted more. Someone made chicken sounds. David held out his glass, and Berlin refilled it from the bottle she had in her hand—Black Bush. The crowd applauded. The sound of the crowd chanting, "Ross! Ross! Ross!" echoed out over the river on the sultry night air.

Chapter 9

The lights had not gone out, the music still played, but the tone at the Greer party had changed as the hour grew late. The music had graduated to techno, and some of the younger, hipper grad student types were dancing to it, trying to prove that not all humanities dorks were moveless.

On the patio, the crowd had dispersed, and only a couple of small groups conversed, unwilling to give up the ghost. A mechanical engineering Ph.D candidate carried his religion major T.A. girlfriend to the edge of the pool and, while she struggled weakly, threw her in. And followed her in to make sure she kept the faith.

In the guest bathroom off Greer's second-floor study, David leaned over the basin and washed his face with cool water. As he buried his face in the towel, drying off, he heard the techno music from downstairs get suddenly louder, then mute again. He looked from beneath the towel into the mirror. Berlin had entered the bathroom.

"I'm done," David said.

She locked the door and leaned back against it. She

was flushed, her hair a little wild from dancing, her eyes interested in what she saw in the bathroom.

David folded the towel and threw it over the rack, watching her a little warily in the mirror.

"I'm not a student anymore," Berlin said.

"Don't think I want to know what that means," David said. He was not a paradigm of sobriety. He turned and leaned back slowly against the sink. They faced each other on opposite sides of the bathroom.

Berlin said:

> There once was a woman named Berlin,
> Who liked a bit now and again.
> Not now and again,
> But Now! And Again!
> And Again! And Again! And Again!

David laughed.

"Cute, huh?" Berlin said.

"Cute," David said.

"I have a secret," Berlin said. "But I have to come over there to tell you."

He made an I'm-not-so-sure face. He made no gesture of welcome but neither did he flee the bathroom. This girl was obviously in a fragile state, he said to himself: Be careful.

She moved playfully toward him. "Here I come," she said.

She went to him, leaning into him as she put her mouth close to his ear. He kept his hands back on the sink counter.

"I wasn't after the grade," Berlin said, whispering. She stood with her body against him, looked into his eyes.

"Berlin, this, this is not . . ." David said.

She put her fingers over his mouth and kept them there. "Sssshhhh," she said. With her free hand she took one of his and rubbed it against her face and lips as she spoke. "We'll just talk, analyze, contemplate," Berlin said. "Or . . . you can just put your mouth on my body."

She moved his hand down, brushing it against her breast and to her groin. She brought her mouth toward her fingers—which were still against his lips.

"Don't reject me," Berlin said, softly, vulnerably. "Please."

With her eyes open, she kissed the back of her own fingers, ran her tongue between them, opening them to reach his mouth.

The handle to the bathroom door rattled. Out in the hallway, a young Latina woman, whose T-shirt read, OTHER, tried the handle a second time. She listened, then shrugged, smiling knowingly. She beebopped back down the hallway, looking for a bathroom that wasn't already booked.

Downstairs in Greer's living room, eight dancers danced to the techno music as its pace increased. A couple of them, deeply stoned, were really into it, oblivious to their surroundings.

A room away in the kitchen, Ross sat at the breakfast table, holding his throbbing head against the pounding music. Greer, the worn-out host, set a cup of coffee in front of him and sat down across the table. They looked at each other blearily. They seemed like parents waiting out a teenager's party.

Berlin and David were oblivious to their setting, and to the awkwardness of what they suddenly found themselves compelled to do against Greer's guestroom sink. Kissing in full passion, they started to disrobe without separating, and not without animal noises, which the pulsing music from downstairs, ever louder, covered nicely.

Berlin's T-shirt was off. Her back against the sink, she undid David's fly as he stripped off his T-shirt. The music kept pace as his trousers and underwear fell to the floor. He moved to penetrate her.

"No," Berlin said. "From behind."

Panting, David turned her against the sink and pulled up her skirt, reaching for her panties.

"Just rip them," Berlin said hoarsely, bent over the marble counter, watching herself in the mirror.

"What?" David said.

"Rip them off," she said.

He did so with one quick motion, positioned himself behind, and entered her.

"Yes," Berlin said.

He moved against her.

"Do it hard," Berlin said.

He looked at her in the mirror, then continued. She watched him.

A floor below, but not far off, one introspective soul sat alone at the side of Greer's patio on a lounger. It was the astrophysicist dude in the Jerry Garcia T-shirt. "Richard Flammang, astrophysicist," were his exact, and practically only, words when he walked in the front door and shook Greer's hand much earlier. Greer didn't know him from Adam, asked if he was at the right party, and handed him a drink anyway. The slender dude said only, "Where's Fritz?" and wandered off. Now the reclining Flammang, listening to a rare Grateful Dead bootleg on his headphones, watched the two dancers moving to that different kind of music in the bathroom above. He wasn't so much watching them as they were the kinetic wallpaper behind his Dead tape from some long-ago legendary concert. His gaze drifted from the primal ballet to the stars overhead.

David thrust against Berlin, her thighs pounded against the edge of the bathroom sink. The music was as loud here as it was downstairs.

"Harder," Berlin gasped.

He looked at her in the mirror, unsure.

"Harder," she said.

He thrust harder.

"Yes," she said.

They continued in rhythm. She reached back and pulled him into her. "Bite me," she said. "Bite my shoulder." She watched him do it in the mirror.

The dancers in the living room careened, the techno pushing them to ever higher energy outbursts. One dancer was a blur.

On the patio, Flammang took a last look at the action below and above and, without a good-bye to anyone, walked away into the night, disappearing in the direction of the river.

Berlin was pulling David into her. Their movements intensified as they approached a climax. She reached backward and grabbed him, scratching him on the small of his back. Blood trickled.

Below, the music and dancers were in pure frenzy. Abruptly, the music stopped. The dancers, stunned by the silence, stopped, looked around. Greer stood by the stereo, removing his hand from the POWER button. "That's all, folks," he said.

Disappointed groans oozed from the sweating partyers.

"Thanks for coming," Greer said.

The dancers looked at each other for a moment as they caught their breath and came down from the place of bacchic fervor. They started to search around for their purses and fanny packs and car keys.

In the silence above, David and Berlin stood still and apart, breathing heavily, suddenly returned to reality. David looked at her in the mirror, a flicker of rue, of shame. She gave him an odd smile.

Chapter 10

Constance Harraway lived alone in a bungalow near the university. It was tidy, attractive, sufficient to the needs of a single woman. Flowers bloomed in planters. Rugs brightened the floors. The porch and walk were swept clean.

Constance had had lovers but never the keeper, the one to play house with, the guy for whom she was willing to give up her independence or divert her energies from her academic career. Was he out there, that compelling but real guy, or was she wedded to a Platonic ideal—the Form of Male Companionableness—next to which the actual tweed-jacketed, self-absorbed schmoes who populated her university world seemed but shadows on the cave wall? She chided herself for being overly analytical when it came to men. She had no choice; cool-eyed analysis was a category of mind hard-wired into the Constance Harraway psyche. Her life was ordered, in control, and lonely.

She woke with a jolt, sweating. Yet the night had cooled, and it wasn't particularly hot in her bedroom. She lay still for a moment, feeling her heart beating.

She got up and walked a little unsteadily, in her sensible cotton pajamas which were now damp with sweat, into the bathroom. She turned on the light, moved to the sink, and reached for the medicine cabinet. Suddenly she turned to the toilet and vomited. She sat back on the floor staring up at the wall, trying to read her body.

The coffeehouse near the U.T. Campus was the real thing: funkytown, not one of those cookie-cutter franchised Starbucks sort of places. It had been there since Joan Baez and Bob Dylan and Willie Nelson actually sang in such venues, since the Days of Rage when college long-hairs fueled up on radicalism and caffeine at the copper urns of local, hippie-run coffee dives. They were the seedbeds of protest, mulch heaps of social conscience.

David and Constance sat at a little round table, the requisite large cappuccino and latte in front of them, fomenting their latter-day brand of protest. David, dressed in a coat and tie and a long face, was distracted. Constance was wearing the closest thing she had to business attire—a long Levi's skirt, blouse, brocaded vest—and had stacks of paper arrayed in front of her.

"Let's say we found an innocent on death row," Constance said. "What would change? After the retrial, the governor would simply go on TV and say, 'See, thanks to the good people at DeathWatch, the system works.' Sure, if we had absolute proof that he had *executed* an innocent, we could demand a moratorium. Like in Illinois. Are you okay?"

He was a DeathWatch role model, the governor of Illinois. In 2000, he had called a halt to all executions for a period of reassessment after thirteen of twenty-five men on death row were found to be innocent.

"Sorry," David said, coming out of his daze. "Yeah." He made an effort to be a "good listener."

"But it won't happen," Constance said. "Dead men can't make a case. And almost-martyrs don't count."

"Got it," David said.

"Keep it rational," Constance said. "The death penalty is expensive and doesn't deter murderers. Quite the opposite. The Texas prison population is growing at twice the national average. . . ."

"Um-hum," David said.

"And stop that," Constance said.

"What?" he said.

"Active listening," Constance said. "I hate active listeners. I always feel they're too busy pretending to listen to actually hear what I'm saying. Did you bring the Amnesty stats?"

"I can listen and appear to listen at the same time," David said. "Yeah—no." He felt in his pockets. "Damn. I left them at home."

"I have a copy," Constance said. She flipped through her papers and found a copy in the stack beneath her coffee cup. She started to hand it to him. He was looking out the window, caught in a thought.

"You want to tell me what's up?" Constance said.

"Nothing," David said. "Everything. Something profoundly stupid happened last night."

"I hope you used a condom," Constance said, teasing.

A beat. His reaction told her the jest had hit home.

"Jesus Christ, David," Constance said. "Was she one of yours?"

A longer beat. He held her eyes. "It was Berlin," he said.

She was stunned, then genuinely angry. "Oh, that's . . . great, great," she said. "I can hear the grapevine now: 'They suspended her so that Gale could dick her with a clear conscience. A power differential equals coercion.' Great. You are so weak."

"Constance, you're not my wife," David said. "Thank God." He was aggravated—and surprised—at the vehemence of her reaction.

"Don't worry. It's not a position I aspire to, believe me," Constance said. "So fuck you." She stood, collecting her papers. She was agitated. She wiped her brow.

"I didn't mean—" David said.

"Let's go," Constance said. As she collected her papers, she breathed in deeply, holding her side.

"Are you okay?" David said.

"Yes, let's go," she said, leading the way into and through the attached bookstore. Businesslike, she carried on briefing him as they walked. "There are seventeen thousand murders a year in the United States," Constance said. "Ten of the twelve states that have abolished the death penalty have a murder rate *lower* than the national average. . . ."

Chapter 11

KQAU in Austin aired public service debates around election time and occasionally at other times when issues of compelling interest came to the fore. In Texas, the busiest death penalty state, with 256 executions since reinstatement, capital punishment was a perennial source of interest and controversy.

To some.

But not everybody cared. The reigning political establishment deemed it a nonstory and did its best to treat the execution of criminals as business as usual, like trash collecting—unpleasant in the details but a social necessity. It was the purging of society of certain toxic undesirables, of individuals whose crimes were so heinous as to make the perpetrators undeserving of the society of man, even under lock and key.

In the TV station control booth, two engineers sat in front of monitors displaying various camera angles on the soundstage. The set was no high-end, computer-console, mission-control broadcast center, but instead had an upscale, regional television look: simple chairs, conference table, moderator's station, all against a photo-mural background of the Austin city skyline. The main monitor was playing the end of the show's opening credits.

"In three, two . . ." the assistant director said into his headset. A camera operator pointed his finger, cueing the host, Alan Michaud.

A fifty-something bow tie–wearing news wonk with a high, intelligent forehead and slicked-back slate hair, Michaud gave off an air of self-satisfied superiority. He was flanked by hypernaturally coifed Governor Hardin—pompadored locks with lots of hairspray to keep the pomp from drooping—and by David Gale, dressed up for the occasion in a twenty-year-old sport jacket and a knit tie. The governor had the rare ability to look comfortable on-camera while David fidgeted just enough to look the opposite.

"Welcome back to *Batter's Box*," the TV host said to the camera. "We continue our very special four-part series with Governor Hardin. Arguing capital punishment with him is DeathWatch codirector Professor David Gale."

"You're up, Governor," host Alan said to Hardin.

"You know, Alan, I always say the same thing," Governor Hardin said. "And I'm gonna keep on sayin' it."

Constance stood behind the cameras. She gestured to David something about the papers in front of him.

"*I hate killin'*," Governor Hardin said. "And my administration will kill to stop it." He was a car salesman with a catchy spiel.

"Murderers are not deterred by the fear of execution," David said. "All two hundred studies on the subject say the same thing." He made an effort to sound matter-of-fact, authoritative, and not as pissed off about the whole thing as he in fact was.

"Well, maybe you should read the Bible," Governor Hardin said. "Deuteronomy 19:21. Eye for an eye. Tooth for a tooth."

"What did Gandhi say?" David said, checking his notes. "The old law of an eye for an eye leaves us all blind."

Constance brightened: One for our side!

"Sorry, but with respect, that's fuzzy liberal thinking," Governor Hardin said.

"With respect, you used it, Governor," David said. "In a speech during your first campaign."

Constance, biting her lip, broke into a smile.

The governor was unsure how to react; then he laughed. The host chuckled with him.

"Well, 'If you're not a liberal at thirty you've got no heart. If you're still a liberal at forty you've got no brain,' " Governor Hardin said. "Winston Churchill."

The host's laughter was overdone. Constance bit her lip again.

"So basically you feel, to choose another quote, that 'A healthy society must stop at nothing to cleanse itself of evil,' " David said.

The governor made an animated, thinking face. "Well, yes, I would have to agree," Governor Hardin said. He chuckled again. "Did I say that too?"

"No, sir," David said. "That was Hitler."

Constance made a "Yes!" gesture with her hands. The governor was making for unusually easy pickings—and David was sharp tonight, she thought gratefully. He was a first-class debater when sharp, but it was not an adjective one could always apply to the David Gale who showed up.

The governor was surprised briefly into silence. Host Alan laughed. But then, noticing Hardin's reaction, trailed off.

"Governor, can't we just admit that capital punishment isn't working," David said. "We've condemned people to death based on phony expert testimony, junk science, jailhouse snitches. Texas has the highest per capita incarceration rate, higher than China . . ."

"Can I get a word . . . Alan, can I get a word in . . . ?" Governor Hardin said.

David charged on: "Forty-three people who you executed were represented by lawyers who had at some point been disbarred or sanctioned—"

"I'm not a lawyer . . ." Governor Hardin said.

The show's producer in the studio control booth smiled. The heat was mounting, the participants were punching, fur was starting to fly—good show. On a bank of monitors, he watched David continue his speech.

"There are two men on death row right now whose lawyers took naps during cross-examination," he said. "In both cases, the Texas Court of Criminal Appeals ruled this wasn't grounds for a retrial."

On the set, it was more than the television lights that was bothering Hardin. He was sweating, irritated by David's polemic.

"It's nuts!" David said. "The system is flawed." David briefly cut his eyes to Constance. He was on a roll, had the cheesehead on the defensive. "And a flawed system will kill innocent men," he said.

Constance's eyes flared. That was a mistake! The governor would be ready for that one.

"All right, Mr. Gale. I'll play your game," Governor Hardin said, suddenly relaxing. "Name one. Name one innocent man that Texas has put to death in my tenure. *One*. Of the hundred or so executions I've presided over—"

"A hundred and thirty-one," David said.

The governor waved his hand dismissively. He pulled out his pen. "Whatever," he said. "Just give me a name. I'll write it down. A man you can *prove* was innocent, and we'll call a moratorium."

A long, miserable beat. The host waited expectantly.

David had set himself up. In other states there had been cases showing probable wrongful executions, but so far none in Texas. Once a man was dead, efforts to exonerate him pretty much died with him.

"Mr. Gale?" the TV host said.

"Dead men can't make a case," David muttered.

The governor unclicked his pen and pocketed it. "Well, as my father used to say, there are enough big problems in the world—no need to scare up small ones."

Constance shook her head in irritation. David knew better. He was pushing it, going for a knockout blow, and instead he carelessly threw up a fat one for the governor to hit out of the park.

The show was over. David and the governor stood and shook hands as Constance stood nearby.

"You had me on the fuckin' Hitler quote," Governor Hardin said.

"Thanks," David said. He did not feel chummy toward this glad-handing pol, and he was particularly hot just now for having blown it to a guy he knew he should have eaten for breakfast.

"These debates make us all look good," Governor Hardin said expansively. "Gotta go." He moved toward his handlers. "You folks keep up the good work," he called back to them. "We need that opposition. Keeps us on our toes. Shows the folks out there that we're doing our jobs." He nodded and waved good-bye amiably. "Mr. Gale," he said. "Ma'am," he said to Constance.

Constance's and David's insincere smiles dropped abruptly as the triumphant governor turned on his way, waving presidentially toward the gantry, where the studio electricians applauded him.

Constance and David walked in depressed silence along the sidewalk toward the parking lot. Constance seethed, and finally she blurted: "Your exact words were," she said, " 'Just tell me when my ego gets in the way of the work.' " She stared at him. "Now I'm telling you: Your ego's getting in the way of the work."

"Look, I wanted you to do this anyway," David said, indicating the TV studio, trying to avoid a fight.

"You put up precisely two seconds of protest at the thought of being in television debates," Constance said.

"What's that supposed to mean?" David said.

"It means that DeathWatch suffers because you're so anxious to finger authority," she said, "to publicly prove that David Gale is so much smarter than the powers that be. Learn to work without an audience, David." She visibly fumed.

The DeathWatch cause meant so much to her, she committed a lot of emotional energy to it. Why didn't everyone else have the same dedication and take the same care she did in pursuing it? David's thumb-your-nose-at-the-big-shots, shoot-from-the-hip style rankled her. It was cowboy. There were lives at stake here. It wasn't a my-dick-is-bigger-than-your-dick contest. "Try squeezing money from the donor list," she said. "Have you licked one single mail-out envelope?"

David looked at her open-eyed, surprised at the edge and personal slant to her remarks, the cascade of not-altogether-related gripes tumbling out all at once. He stopped, about to respond—ready first to inquire, ever so delicately, if she was feeling all right or if something larger were bothering her. At the same moment, two gray suits standing at the end of the sidewalk caught his eye. They appeared to be waiting for them.

"Mr. Gale?" a Latino man said.

"Look, guys," David said, assuming they were newsmedia, "there's not much more to say. . . ."

"Ramirez, Austin Police," the man said. He gestured toward his Anglo, thirtyish partner. "This is Officer Haslinger."

The two officers flipped open their IDs. Constance took one to examine it more closely.

"What," David said, "arguing with the governor is a crime?"

"No, sir, rape is," Haslinger said.

Constance and David looked at each other, stunned. But in a nanosecond, David flushed all over as his mind flashed to a scene that, no matter how hard he wished, he would never be able to undo.

Chapter 12

On weekdays, the death row visitation area in Ellis Unit rarely had more than one or two families or visiting groups at a time. During the two hours Bitsey had been there, no one else had come in or out. She had been able to listen to David Gale's recitation uninterruptedly. He was a good talker; he stuck to the through line, with none of the "Oh, and let me tell you about the time . . ." digressions one might have expected from the long-incarcerated. He did not, to be sure, have forever. Like the trained university lecturer he was, he had planned what he wanted to say, organized it carefully, and delivered it masterfully. His audience of one was captivated. Bitsey had been taking notes steadily but almost unconsciously, unaware of how long she'd been there.

"Gale, time's up," the supervising guard blared over the loudspeaker.

The voice, as loud as ever, startled Bitsey. She reflexively looked at her watch, then checked it against the clock on the wall.

David nodded toward the guard, acknowledging his announcement, and hastened to finish this first part of his story. "Berlin had bite marks, bruises, ripped clothing," he said. "My skin was beneath her nails. It didn't look like anything but rape. Then she dropped the case and left town. It looked like I was guilty and that she was too traumatized to face a trial. My wife got to read about it as she waited at the airport, wondering why I wasn't there to meet her. It was two weeks before she bailed me out."

"And the grad student Berlin?" Bitsey said. "Why'd she do it?"

The door guard approached. David stood up and moved to the back of his cage, put his hands behind him and out the slot in the back. The guard snapped the handcuffs on him.

"Give the finger to authority?" he said. "Show she was smarter than the powers that had expelled her? Grad student's revenge? I really don't know."

"Do you know where I can find her?" Bitsey said.

"My first year in here I received a postcard from San Francisco," David said. "It was signed: *Berlin, the student who would do anything*." Cuffed now, he stood aside for the cage door to be opened.

"What else did she say?" Bitsey said.

"Only: *I'm sorrier than you can know*," David said. He stood and looked at her until the guard gave him a poke.

"Move it, Gale," the door guard said.

"I'm running out of time," David said matter-of-factly. He turned and walked out of the cage back toward his solitary cell. To his home for three more days.

Time was almost concrete to him now, six more spins of the clock. What was an abstraction to him most of his life now felt like a fast-flowing river

pushing him toward a waterfall. After refusing for
six years to give out his own story for public con-
sumption, he had arranged to tell it at the very last.
Three sessions had seemed like plenty of time when
he arranged it; now the river seemed to be picking
up speed and hurtling him toward the edge.

Freedom was sitting outside a greasy, two-bit
steakhouse smelling the aroma of Texas cow flesh
charbroiling on a cooling but still muggy summer
night. To David Gale the charcoal smoke would have
been an exotic perfume. To Bitsey and Zack, the giant
steaks flaming on the dripping iron grill behind the
counter were just a guilty indulgence at the end of
an oddly stressful, tiring day.

Zack got up from the outdoor table, walked
through the smoky night air, and picked up their
order from the takeout window.

"Can you imagine his wife letting him stew in jail
for two weeks?" he said as he put down Bitsey's and
his dinners on the wooden table.

"Who can blame her?" Bitsey said.

It was clear who was identifying with whom.

"Get an address for the Berlin girl from the university," Bitsey said as she bit into her T-bone and
chewed, relishing it somewhat less than she had expected. Gents in Stetsons and women with hair piled
high to keep it off their perspiring necks ate beef at
surrounding tables. Almost without exception they
drank longnecks, the Texas state wine, perfect with
steer. Willie Nelson twanged his guitar and sang
"Help Me Make It Through the Night" in the
background.

"You still don't think he's telling the truth?" Zack

said. He was only half in the conversation, gazing around, basking in the down-and-Western authenticity of the whole scene, so starkly different from Upper West Side Manhattan.

"On the Berlin rap?" Bitsey said.

"On the whole rap," Zack said, coming back to focus.

Bitsey and Zack walked across the steakhouse parking lot, the lights of one of the ten local prisons glowing in the distance. High institutional walls with razor-wire crowns loomed over every compass point of the low-slung small town. For the locals, the prisons, though not much talked about—unless one of your family worked in one—were rarely completely out of sight and never out of mind. They were by far the town's largest employer.

Zack, although he'd never own up to it, was a little spooked by this universe of detention and doom— by its ubiquity. It made him uneasy to think of the many thousands of locked-up, angry, despairing and surely desperate men and women stewing behind walls that seemed to loom everywhere. Terrible karma, a place like this, he thought, an American gulag. Out of the direct vision of "good folks," such a place was nonetheless deemed paramount to the general safety, unavoidable if a sane, orderly society was the goal. But how could these people live in this town without being affected by it, one way or another? Zack mused. Had he grown up here, he was sure, he'd've spent his youth plotting to escape at the earliest possible moment.

Huntsville denizens who went elsewhere found that their place of origin was both recognizable and notorious, not just in Texas but throughout the Southwest. Anytime a new arrival in another town said they were from Huntsville, residents automatically wondered if he or she had done time inside, or if a relative had. Did his or her family earn their living in the place, and did they, in effect, smell of it? It was like a minor scarlet letter that a Huntsville native had to wear around his neck wherever he went, a credential he or she had to live with or live down.

"Do I still think he's not telling the truth? Who knows?" Bitsey said, continuing the conversation about Gale they'd interrupted earlier, by mutual consent, in order to eat their steaks free of unpalatable thoughts. "Anyway, there is no truth, only perspectives."

"Can't say that," Zack said promptly. "If you say, 'There is no truth,' you're claiming that it's *true* that there is no truth. It's a logical contradiction." He grinned. College Logic 101.

"Working on our philosophy merit badge, are we, Zack?" Bitsey said dryly.

"When it comes to rape," Zack said, "an accusation is as good as a conviction. It sticks like shit."

"That's an appetizing metaphor," Bitsey said.

"Technically, a simile," Zack said. "*I* think he's telling the truth."

"This you know from sitting in the prison lobby?" Bitsey said.

"It's just my perspective," Zack said.

She opened the rental car door. "Three different courts found him guilty, Zack," she said. "That's enough perspective for me."

They got into the car and belted up, unaware that they were being watched.

In a dark corner of the parking lot sat the long gray crew-cab pickup from the rest area. The Cowboy watched Bitsey and Zack make their preparations. He moved his head slightly in time to the music—Puccini's "Un Bel Di" from *Madame Butterfly*—that played on his truck's CD player. He put the truck into gear and followed slowly as the rental car pulled out of the steakhouse parking lot.

Chapter 13

Wednesday was to be their second full day in Texas, and the second installment of David Gale's story as told to Bitsey Bloom, National Correspondent, *NEWS Magazine*. A story, even an interview, from just one source was a story without context, credibility, or authority. Bitsey was as good as the best at putting a story into a three-dimensional human context, demonstrating its credibility and framing it with authority.

Austin was west-southwest of Huntsville, not far as the crow flies, but no limited-access turnpike ran between them. Texas state byroads were the only way to go, 155 miles of small towns and crossroads with names like Roans Prairie and Navasota. It was a slow, though occasionally pretty drive, into the Texas Hill Country, some of the greenest, most scenic landscapes in Texas.

Austin wasn't known just as the state capital or just as the main campus of the state university system—or even just for its ever-vital country and blues music scene. It was known too for its individualistic people, a population of self-willed eccentrics who marched to their own Fender Stratocasters.

One of the Austin stories that *NEWS Magazine* covered the previous year had nothing to do with murder or David Gale or Texas football, but it did have to do with the law. Kruger's back-of-the-book legal section did a short item on a liability case that had local people chuckling or fuming, depending which side of the fence they leaned on.

A jury in Austin saw fit to award one of its own—Kathleen Robertson—$780,000 after she broke her ankle tripping over a toddler running inside a furniture store. The owners of the store took issue with the verdict, inasmuch as the toddler was Ms. Robertson's own son. An appeal was pending.

" 'Check out the crime scene in Austin.' You made it sound so close," Bitsey groused. She had the passenger seat fully reclined and lay with her eyes closed as they drove into the city at last. "Shit, 2.5 hours." She stretched uncomfortably and looked at her watch.

Once in the city, though, they were close to where they wanted to go; everywhere was close in Austin. Zack drove them down past the capitol, then followed signs up to the University. From there it was supposed to be five minutes to the neighborhood they sought.

The rental car moved slowly through an older Austin residential suburb with well-kept wood-framed houses from the 1950s. They continued farther into a part of the neighborhood that had gone downhill. Once-charming cottages were now in various states of disrepair, the lawns unkempt. Paint peeled from garage doors, and furniture sat in front yards. The overcast day didn't add any cheer to the depressed surroundings.

"Thirty-three-o-what?" Zack said.

"Seven," Bitsey said.

"Bitsey," Zack said. She brought her seatback up and sat up. She looked out the side window.

Zack was pointing at a gray clapboard bungalow that needed paint, sitting back from the street on a small plot that needed a gardener. In front of the house a homemade sign read:

> DAVID GALE DEATH HOUSE AND MUSEUM.
> SEE WHERE IT HAPPENED!

Beneath the sign were the opening hours: 12–8 P.M." Someone had X-ed out the hours and instead scribbled, *Ring bell.*

Bitsey and Zack shared a look, amazed at the sign: amazed that it was there in the first place, surprised that it was still there so many years after the event. They parked at the curb in front of the house. There was not a lot of competition for the space. They walked up the walk, looking around at the semiseedy neighborhood, a little leery of what they might be sticking their noses into.

They mounted the porch. Paint cracked and flaked from the pillars; the floorboards were scraped down to the bare wood. Bitsey rang the bell.

Zack stomped out a cigarette. Raising his eyebrows, he pointed out a worn BLOCK HOME sign in the window.

As Bitsey straightened out her skirt, the door swung open. A Goth Girl, not quite eighteen by her looks, looked at them inquiringly. She had chopped-off jet-black hair, nose and lip piercings, tattoos, and a black-on-black Marilyn Manson T-shirt over a body carrying forty pounds excess weight. Metal music came from within.

Goth Girl just looked at them, waiting.

Bitsey processed the tattered Madonna-gone-black outfit and the silver mucus-membrane studs. After an uncomfortable silence, she extended her hand to the girl. "Hi. I'm Bitsey Bloom and this is Zack Stemmons. We—"

"You want the tour?" Goth Girl said. When she spoke, her tongue stud glittered.

"Uh, yes," Bitsey said.

"There's a twenty-dollar mandatory donation, apiece," the Goth Girl said. "But you get a reenactment photo packet. It's got five pictures." She looked off over their heads, waiting. Eye contact wasn't her thing.

"Okay," Bitsey said.

Goth Girl stood there in the doorway. Bitsey and Zack couldn't move forward. "I gotta collect first," the girl in black said.

"Oh, sure," Bitsey said. Bitsey reached into her purse and came up with forty dollars of *NEWS Magazine*'s money. It would go on her expense report just as it happened: "Two death house tour admissions, reenactment photos included, Austin, TX."

They entered the dark, messy living room. A shabby green velveteen couch and a TV/VCR opposite dominated the space, along with two small hardback chairs and an end table barely big enough to hold two ashtrays filled with butts and the burned ends of rolling papers.

Bitsey noted the details, unobtrusively pulling out her long, narrow reporter's notebook and jotting things down. Goth Girl noticed and couldn't have cared less. She scuffed her way over to the couch and planted herself on the back, watching the gawkers gawk.

Bitsey crossed the room, passing the door to the adjacent kitchen. The living room walls were adorned with Goth iconography: a London Batcave poster, a couple of fanzine pictures of Siouxsie and the Banshees. In a far corner, a dead ficus drooped. To Bitsey it was all gold. The story was already a bit stranger than she'd expected at the beginning. But then the first thing she'd learned as a journalist aeons ago was never to assume, never to write a story in your head before you reported it because you'd always be wrong.

Goth Girl turned down the music and moved to a table near the door that was covered with numbered black-and-white photographs beneath a torn and curling sheet of plastic. Piled on one side of the table were small packets of snapshots along with a few hand-labeled videos and a book of news clippings. Goth Girl spun an open guest book around and pointed to it.

"You gotta sign the book," she said. "Doesn't have to be your real name, though."

Bitsey signed in. She was about to ask why it was necessary, but Goth Girl was way ahead of her. "First page says you're here to do research on violent crime," she said. "The state requires it for nonprofit shit."

Zack signed in.

"Take a reenactment photo packet," Goth Girl said.

Bitsey did so. Zack picked one up, too, and was about to open his.

"If you guys could share one, it would be really cool," their host said. "The fuckers where I do the prints kinda jerk my chain."

Zack put back his packet.

Bitsey was looking at a photo: a female in panties and bra lying on the floor with plastic wrap over her head. She was handcuffed and wearing a platinum-blond wig. It took Bitsey a few moments to realize the girl in the photo was Goth Girl herself. The pose was half corpse, half pinup.

"That's me," Goth Girl said. "My boyfriend took it. We also got a video. It's fifty bucks 'cause you can see my tits. There's a version without tits—that's thirty-five."

"Do many people take the tour?" Bitsey said.

"Not so much anymore," Goth Girl said. "We thought this would be like a busy week—Gale gettin' the prune juice and all." She mimed a hypodermic needle going into the arm. "Prune juice is what death row dudes call the poison 'cause it gives you the shits," Goth Girl said. "Most jerks just take a photo from the street. They shot a *Real Crimes* episode here, but the landlord didn't give us dick."

"You don't mind living here?" Zack said.

"Beats livin' with my dickwad parents," Goth Girl said. "It starts over here." She led them to the coffee table.

Among her own things—an open paperback, a cigarette pack, some loose CDs—was a dusty Black Bush Irish whiskey bottle. Beside it sat a tumbler with an index card labeled #1 leaning against it. The area had been outlined on the table with white shoe polish.

"She let him crash here sometimes," Goth Girl said. "He was, like, constantly wasted. Drank Black Bush religiously."

Bitsey and Zack exchanged a look. Well, this *was* what they came for—other angles on the Gale story—

though the reliability of the source left something to be desired.

Goth Girl shuffled into the kitchen. It was cluttered and dirty except for several areas outlined in white shoe polish and indexed. These were kept clear. The accompanying index cards were smudged and filthy.

Bitsey circled the kitchen, glancing through the windows—they couldn't have been washed in years—and the sliding-glass door that led onto the patio. The backyard hadn't been mowed in months. Twenty or so pots with dead plants lay around. Just inside the door, a triangle of three small taped Xs marked the floor, each outlined and each indexed with #2.

"This is where the tripod was," Goth Girl said. "My boyfriend borrowed the one we usually show to folks. They never found a camera, photos, or videos or anything. Gale must have buried them. These serial killer dudes take photos to whack off to later."

"He's not exactly a serial killer," Zack said.

"Whatever," Goth Girl said. She slouched against the refrigerator and waited for questions.

Bitsey and Zack just looked. On the cracked, faded linoleum floor, the position of Constance's body had been outlined in chalk and labeled #3. In the same area was a pair of handcuffs, marked #4. A few feet away was a roll of duct tape—#5. A pair of latex kitchen gloves lay crumpled on the sink counter. They could well have been just a pair of working gloves but they too were marked—#6.

"She was, like, totally naked right here," Goth Girl said, gesturing. "The meter man saw her through the door. Gale handcuffed her, taped her mouth, then taped a bag over her head so she couldn't breathe.

My boyfriend says that's probably when he fucked her. Your muscles tense up as you die—the sex is better."

She pointed. "He used those housewife gloves so he wouldn't leave prints," Goth Girl said. "They found sticky stuff from the tape on them."

Zack picked up the gloves.

"We ask folks not to touch the exhibit," Goth Girl said. Polite as a docent at the Metropolitan Museum of Art.

"Right," Zack said. He put them back on the counter near the sink, trying to arrange them as he'd found them.

"The totally sick part was where they found the key to the handcuffs," Goth Girl said.

"We know. You can save that," Bitsey said.

"What? Where was it?" Zack said.

"It was in her stomach, dude," Goth Girl said. "He made her swallow it before he bagged her."

Zack, despite himself, was genuinely shocked. Bitsey didn't bat an eye, just listened to the girl.

"That's pretty much the highlights," the girl said. She scratched her left breast through her T-shirt. "Got questions?"

The drive back to Huntsville seemed shorter, partly because both travelers were lost in thought, mired in the grimy details of the crime scene. Goth Girl and her odd, tawdry attempt at squeezing a living out of the Constance Harraway murder added a layer of distaste to the experience that did not leave the New Yorkers in chatty moods.

It was not until they pulled in for a late lunch at a roadside hamburger stand near Huntsville that they

discussed anything about their morning. The rest of
the outdoor tables were empty as they put their trays
down. Zack was too upset to eat. He lit up and
smoked, standing ten feet away from Bitsey blowing
smoke in the opposite direction.

Bitsey sat and began eating her burger, not trying
to hide her disdain for Zack's weak stomach. "It was
in the case file," she said.

"Fuck!" Zack said. "In her stomach? That's cold."

Between bites, Bitsey noticed something down the
road. "Zack," she said.

"What?" Zack said.

"Look," Bitsey said. She pointed with her burger.
The Cowboy's big crew-cab pickup was parked at
the side of the two-lane highway, about half a mile
away. It was too far away to see if he was inside it.

"Isn't that the cowboy from the rest area?" Bitsey
said.

"Same truck," Zack said.

"Weird coincidence, huh?" Bitsey said.

"Coincidences are always weird," Zack said.
"That's why they're coincidences." The remark was
a little flippant, but Zack wasn't feeling all that flip.
Why in God's name would somebody be following
them on this story? What possible damage could he
and Bitsey do? So they were talking with David
Gale—who could care? Gale was pretty much of a
dead letter already, Zack thought, taking no pleasure
in the pun.

Chapter 14

Interview two with Ellis Unit inmate number 4178694 was to take place in the same visitation area as the day before. It was a Wednesday, two days before David Gale's scheduled execution on Friday at six p.m.

As she waited in the prison anteroom to be admitted, Bitsey read background file clippings from *NEWS Magazine*'s morgue and cogitated on the idea of knowing one's exact date of death beforehand. She tried to imagine knowing she had just two days to live, tried to picture how she would handle it. She would be screaming around the walls, tearing her hair out, she figured, and she would require industrial doses of horse tranquilizers and other somas.

She knew from one of the background clips that prior notice of one's execution date wasn't standard in other places, nor was public notice. In Japan, one of the few other Westernized countries still to use capital punishment, executions were conducted in secrecy. It was unheard of for a convicted murderer to know in advance the day he was going to die. There, inmates were informed they were about to be executed just minutes beforehand. They were allowed time to clean their cells, write a final letter, and receive last rites. Relatives were not told until after the prisoner was hanged, and then they had twenty-four hours to collect the body. If they didn't act quickly, the body was cremated.

It was the only humane way to do it, Japanese Justice Ministry officials said, a gesture of kindness. Knowing beforehand, "the condemned would lose themselves to despair," one official was quoted as saying. "They might even try to commit suicide or escape."

On the contrary, the practice is acutely inhumane, according to an inmate who had spent thirty-four years on death row in Japan before his conviction was set aside and he was released. He spoke about the "severe anguish," "intense foreboding," and "excruciating uncertainty" that prisoners experienced from not knowing. Day after day, for a thirty- to forty-minute period each morning during execution season, the halls of death row grew eerily quiet. Prisoners barely dared breathe as they waited to see if the wardens were going to stop in front of their cells. When no warden came, they knew they had another day to live. Such intense stress "was part of a system to make us docile," the ex-prisoner was quoted as saying, and it was in fact "unbearably cruel."

Bitsey was led in to see David Gale, who not only knew the date and time he would meet his Maker, but exactly how many minutes of each of his final three full days he would devote to revealing his side of his tragic story. It was a strange arrangement, Bitsey thought, however she parsed it. Why had he waited so long? Why just one correspondent? Why these three short, equal sessions?

She sat opposite David—and realized with a flash

that she indeed now thought of him as "David" and not "Gale." She noted as much in her notebook.

She also noted quickly that he seemed less animated than on the previous day, drained. He rubbed his wrists. He started off by speaking in hushed tones.

"Off the record?" David said.

"All right, we're off," Bitsey said. She clicked her pen demonstratively.

"Constance was murdered by what's called the Securitat Method," he said. "You're handcuffed, forced to swallow the key, taped at the mouth, a bag's sealed over your head, and you're left to suffocate. The Securitat did this to Romanians who wouldn't inform or confess. Sometimes the bag was ripped off at the last second, and you got a second chance. If not, you died knowing the 'key' to your freedom was inside you the whole time. A cheap, but effective, metonym. Problem is, I once mentioned the method in an article. The prosecution never knew."

Bitsey knew what a metonym was: a figure of speech in which an attribute or feature of a thing is used to designate the thing with which it is closely associated, like "the crown" standing for "the king" or a "hired gun" meaning a "contract killer." Curious, she thought, that he would use a literary device at such a time. Despite his dire straits and the incredible stress he must be feeling, he still had the ability to stand back and look at the whole situation with a surprising degree of abstraction and calm.

"Someone's framing you?" she said.

"It's more than that," David said.

Bitsey waited. She was a master of the fruitful wait—the silent nonresponse, the intentional, awkward emptiness a skillful questioner leaves out there with the expectation that the interviewee will eventually fill it. The only cure for an awkward silence was continuing talk and elaboration. Simple expectant silence was a good reporter's oldest, best technique.

"There was a tripod," David said.

"Right, facing her body," Bitsey said. "Are we back on the record?"

David nodded.

Bitsey clicked her pen. She wasn't at all clear why, at this late date, he cared that the Securitat material was off the record.

"Not a single print was found on it," David said. "Someone brought the tripod, wiped it, left it. Why? It's as if they wanted me to know that somewhere there's a record of what really happened that afternoon. As if they wanted me to die knowing the key to *my* freedom was . . . out there."

"Maybe you're being paranoid?" Bitsey said. Or maybe just fanciful and overly dramatic, she thought but didn't say.

"Ms. Bloom, I'm the state's leading death penalty abolitionist and I'm on death row," David said. "Doesn't that strike you as odd?"

"Any ideas who 'they' are?" Bitsey said.

"No," David said.

A silence. Bitsey just watched him.

"But I have someone on it," David said, "someone I'm relying on to prove my innocence."

"Belyeu's hired a detective?" Bitsey said.

He shook his head. "A journalist," he said. "She has to help me."

It took Bitsey a second to understand that he meant her. She gave him a pointedly neutral look.

"You know I'm innocent," David said.

"No . . . no, I don't," Bitsey said.

They both sensed she was lying. He gave her the smile. He took a long breath, leaned back, and switched into his storytelling tone.

"Sharon finally left me," he said.

Chapter 15

The day David Gale's wife left was a quiet Saturday.
He was working in his office on the U.T. campus,
trying to make sense of undergraduate term papers
for his 389 seminar, "Philosophical Horizons in Science: The God Problem." He was knitting his brows
over a valiant student attempt to use the cumulative
efficaciousness of inductive reasoning as cudgel
against the Primum Mobile argument for God, when
Sharon called him on her cell phone. She was in her
jeep outside—could he come out?

A few students crisscrossed the campus as David
came down the steps from Blackwell Hall. The football stadium loomed in the background, empty at
this time of year. The humanities faculty parking lot
contained a scattered handful of cars as well as
Sharon and Jamie, who stood near the Jeep. David
could see suitcases piled in the back.

Immediately and visibly upset, he walked toward
them. Jamie ran out to him, carrying his stuffed
sheep, Cloud Dog. He jumped on his dad.

"Wear me like a fur, Daddy!" Jamie said. "Wear
me like a fur!"

As he walked, David draped the boy sideways over his shoulders like a fur stole. Jamie squealed with pleasure. "Who's your hero?" David said.

Jamie bonked him on the nose.

David set Jamie down when he reached Sharon. He kissed Jamie good-bye as the boy struggled to move on to something else.

A long moment as David and Sharon stood, uncomfortable.

"Call me when you land?" David said.

She nodded, saying nothing, as though just waiting to get this over with.

"Has any couple ever survived a trial separation?" David said. "Isn't the whole idea of separating counter to working things—"

"Don't," Sharon said, interrupting him. Her manner was stony; she was way past discussing things. She turned to Jamie, who was by the Jeep. "Jamie, get in, sweetie," Sharon said.

The driver's-side door was open. Jamie climbed in and sat in the driver's seat. "See ya later, alligator," Jamie said, turning to his dad, his tiny hands on the steering wheel.

"After a while, crocodile," David said.

"Take it easy, Japa-nee-zeee," Jamie said. He waggled the wheel back and forth.

"Okey-dokey, artichokey," David said.

"Scoot," Sharon said to Jamie, ready to get in. Jamie moved over to the passenger seat and Sharon slid into the driver's seat.

"I sent you an e-mail," Sharon said.

"An e-mail?" David said.

"Just read it," Sharon said. Cold, flat, unpleasant. She closed the door.

Suddenly, Jamie opened the passenger-side door and ran around the Jeep carrying Cloud Dog. He ran to David, hugged him one last time.

"Come on, sweetie," Sharon said, cracking her window.

Jamie started to go back, then turned and handed Cloud Dog to his father without comment. He quickly ran back around the Jeep and got inside.

David watched the Jeep drive away. Jamie's hand waved out the window until the vehicle was out of the parking lot. David made himself turn away and start back toward his dismal swamp of student essays.

With sick foreboding, David returned to his office and sat before his computer screen. He couldn't bring himself to go on-line. He got up and closed his office door. He sat back down and, resigned, signed on. He knew what he was going to be reading, but until he saw it in black-and-white, it wasn't quite real.

The computer screen showed his wife's e-mail message:

DAVID, THIS ISN'T A TRIAL. I WANT A DIVORCE. I'M
SORRY I DIDN'T SAY IT BEFORE, BUT BECAUSE I'M
LEAVING THE COUNTRY THERE ARE UNCOMFORT-
ABLE CUSTODY ISSUES.

It went on, but the rest became a blur.

David sat at the computer, staring into space. All the life drained out of him; his bones softened. He barely avoided slumping to the floor, grasping the edge of the desk at the last second to hold on. Slowly he became aware how scruffy and cramped the office around him was. Dirty yellow paint on every surface. The books that lined the walls and filled the desk were inert objects, dead, just so much clutter. On the walls, the framed Peter Black–type poster of Socrates, Freud, and Saussure could have shown the Three Stooges, for all it meant to him. A large, yellowing *New York Times* portrait of Clarence Darrow looked down on him accusingly. Guilty, guilty, guilty, he heard himself say nonsensically. He reached into his desk for a bottle of Black Bush, pulled out the grimy glass that was rolling around in the drawer, and poured it full.

There was a knock on the door and it opened before he could say yea or nay. Constance entered. "You could at least hide the bottle," she said, collapsing onto the broken-backed couch opposite his desk, exhausted.

"Well?" David said. He turned and closed the e-mail and turned back.

"Officially, you're on sabbatical," Constance said. "Unofficially, they want you out of here. It was four to two." She looked tired and beaten, as though she were the one disgraced.

He absorbed the information. "How did Ross vote?" he said at last.

"I'm not supposed to discuss . . . Against you," Constance said.

David nodded.

"And you?" David said.

"*For* you," Constance said. "And against my politics."

"Thanks," David said. He finished his drink and chucked the glass into the drawer.

They both stared into space in silence. He was far

from believing this was actually happening to him. Lost his wife, his child taken away. Lost his job and income. Did he have a reputation still as a fine teacher, useful colleague, productive thinker in his field? All eclipsed, he knew, by the rape charge, the scarlet R that now hung on his resume. His hard-earned, carefully constructed career—the books he'd written, the papers he'd published in scholarly journals, the dull conferences he'd suffered through—his shining career was a wounded duck at best, a dead one possibly. All he could think to do was go someplace and drink and disappear.

Chapter 16

A real estate agent put a FOR SALE sign in the front yard of the Gale home on Orchid Street. The big brick-and-white-clapboard family house in a lovely, leafy neighborhood was as handsome a house as David's academic's salary had been able to support. The giant oaks along the frontage kept the house and lawns cool in the ferocious Texas summer heat. A sixty-foot-long rope swing swayed invitingly in the towering silver maple in the backyard, rigged there for Jamie by his father. In one corner of the yard was a redwood playhouse on stilts, also built for Jamie—and other dreamed-of children. In another corner was a charming bougainvillea-covered gazebo by a goldfish pond. It was a splendid house for anyone with kids. It would sell in a minute.

But heavily mortgaged, it would not yield much capital for the owners upon sale. Almost all of that, by David's wishes, would go to Sharon and his son.

David had found a $420-a-month apartment in a not-so-leafy neighborhood on the far side of the University near the interregional highway. Expressway noise was constant and uniform, so he quickly got used to it. The mildewy smell in his three rooms was harder to ignore, however, and left him feeling slightly nauseated. The view from his living room window was the back side of a shopping center.

His books were stacked and dumped everywhere, obscuring the fact that he had very little furniture: the couch from his office, a Formica-topped table, a claw-footed easy chair he'd taken from his study in his house. He had laid a Turkish kilim diagonally across the living room, hoping to hide the wall-to-wall shag. His computer sat on the same scarred ship-lathe pine desk he'd dragged around with him since graduate school. It no longer gave him the comfort and assurance it once had.

He stood on the narrow balcony of the apartment holding the phone to his ear. He looked down on a communal pool area, where a horribly tanned man in his seventies wearing a Speedo attempted to do tai chi amid barbecue smoke from a three-wheeled grill. A Vietnamese family with two little children kept to themselves in one corner of the courtyard, eating from cartons. A young Hispanic couple necked in the shallow end of the pool.

"Hello," David said into the phone, enunciating carefully. "My name is David Gale."

He listened.

"Gale," David said. "May I speak to Sharon Gale?"

He heard the voice of a Spanish maid on the other end. Then he heard Sharon's voice in Spanish telling the maid to hang up. The line went dead.

"Hello?" David said. He waited, then clicked the phone off and stood looking down at the tai chi performer. His eyes watered, mostly from the barbecue smoke.

*   *   *

Houston was a hundred sixty miles across the interstate but a world away from Austin. It was a big, tough international oil city, an impersonal metropolis compared to hospitable, Hill Country Austin. It was industrialized, commercialized, and worldly, and David thought he'd have better luck finding a job there than in parochial Austin.

David had become infamous in Austin, a poster boy for power differential sexual abuse. Feminists waved the flag on Berlin's behalf, hurrying to all the media outlets that would give them a forum. For weeks at the time of David's arrest and arraignment, his name and purported crime fed the radio talk shows and local TV issues forums. It was major news that a big man on campus like Dr. David Gale should stoop so low, should take such cruel advantage of a hapless girl grad student who was down on her luck. It was downright Clintonian, the local branch of the Vast Right Wing Conspiracy kept repeating. When Berlin abruptly left town before the trial and the charges against David were dropped, the air went out of the media balloon. Local media printed or aired brief stories about the dismissal of the case and gave pro-forma lip service to David's innocence— read *unproven guilt*. The damage was done. There were other universities in Austin, but Dr. David Gale was now tainted meat.

He'd arranged to meet Professor Kroll for lunch in an off-campus restaurant in downtown Houston. Kroll, a displaced Ivy Leaguer in his fifties, had been ten minutes late, and the waiter had managed only water, bread, and butter so far for their table.

"So I wanted to get your feedback on the idea," David said.

Kroll vigorously buttered his bread. "Look, Professor Gale," he said. "I could sit here, and I'm sure others have, and plead departmental cutbacks." He bit into his roll. "Claim you need more publications, or I need a minority, whatever. All bull-*geschichte*. Your record's brilliant. You're an original voice worth—in the scarcity-defines-value capitalist system under which we toil—your weight in gold. Hell, it's not even your alcohol problem. It'd be nice to have a faculty member whose crutch wasn't Prozac. But to speak plainly"—he swallowed his roll—"if I were to hire you, in the eyes of the regents, alumni, and every freshman with an ear for gossip, I'd be hiring a rapist." He buttered more bread and started chewing on it.

"But the charges were dropped," David said.

"People will say you had a good lawyer," Kroll said, smiling.

"I was innocent," David said.

"You don't get it, do you?" Kroll said. "You're not politically correct, Dr. Gale." He looked at David with a can't-fight-city-hall shrug. "Welcome to the club."

It was a depressing drive back to Austin, his home that was no longer home. The news on the job front was worse than David thought if the eminent Professor Kroll felt he didn't even have to couch his "Not a chance—get lost" in the usual gentle euphemisms. The notion that there might no longer be room at the inn of his life's work was devastating. It was a brick wall. He drove past the turnoff to his apartment once he reached Austin and continued on through West Lake Hills and up Lake Austin and the Colorado River. He drank from the bottle in his glove compartment the whole way, unmoved and unsoothed despite the pleasant surroundings, until he felt benumbed enough to go home and go to bed.

Daytime sober but with a two-day stubble, David forced himself out the door and to the supermarket. He didn't look good by any measure. He went through the motions robotically, laying in the bare minimum for bodily needs. He stared straight ahead, seeing no one, making no eye contact as he shopped, went through the line, paid, walked out to the parking lot.

He got into his Volvo, holding a bag of groceries. He sat with the groceries partially obscuring his face for some minutes. Finally he put them down on the seat next to him and pulled his cell phone from his jacket pocket. He dialed a series of numbers and waited. "*Quiero hablar con mi hijo,*" he said. "I want to speak with my son."

An angry male voice answered in Spanish on the other end of the line. It went on heatedly, but David shouted over him, "Let me speak to my son!"

At that moment, a sorority pledge, a girl dressed in a goofy combination of men's and children's clothing with Greek letters painted on her cheek, dashed out from behind a van and took David's picture with a digital flash camera. She ran to a waiting convertible, where two other girls sat. "I got it! I got it!" the sorority pledge said, as the convertible peeled away, the girls laughing.

David sat frozen, breathing hard, staring at the dead phone in his hand.

There were other fish in the sea, other seas to fish, David repeated to himself, mantralike, as he descended the steps from his apartment. People changed careers all the time these days: business people going over to academia and vice versa. He was part of the new fluid work world, Versatile Man, a multitalented, multitasking individual able to respond to the changing conditions of a Global Economy.

Bullshit, he thought. I'm a one-trick pony who just lost his gig and I'm desperate to find another—any other. He was on his way to an interview for a job he'd never given a moment's thought to, except to wonder how people could do such dull stuff for a living.

He parked underneath the downtown high-rise office building in Austin. He rode up in the elevator, looking at himself in the mirrored walls and tightening the knot on his tie as the car reached the eleventh floor. The doors slid open. He gathered himself and walked across to the receptionist.

The office of the V.P. Sales and Development was Philippe Starke chic with floor-to-ceiling windows. The city of Austin lay beyond in the distance. David sat on a sofa across from the ultrasoigné, buxom blond executive who had introduced herself as Angela Ware and ushered him in. The attractive Ms. Ware was somewhere in her thirties, or maybe her forties, it was impossible to tell from her very smooth face. Her big round eyes took David in: not bad, they seemed to say, not an unappealing candidate for the exec training program.

David couldn't take his eyes off the view of Austin that stretched away for miles beyond the tall windows.

"What exactly attracts you most to the bond market?" Ms. Ware said.

David was staring out the window—at nothing and everything, just out.

"Mr. Gale?" Ms. Ware said.

He suddenly looked at her.

She forced a strained smile.

In the dark of the apartment in the middle of the night, the only sounds were the beeps of phone buttons being punched, then a busy signal. Then the same sounds repeated—the beeping, the busy signal. David lay on the floor, his head propped up against a wall. He was wearing only his underwear and drinking from a Black Bush bottle. The phone was at his ear and a far-off busy signal buzzed out of the receiver. He closed his eyes and listened to it for a while. He opened his eyes and hung up, waited for a dial tone, and punched redial. He got another busy signal. He listened and took a drink. After a while he hung up, got a dial tone, and punched redial. Busy signal. He went through the whole sequence again. He would do it long into the night, until he passed out.

Chapter 17

Radio Shack had a nice new store in the strip mall behind David's apartment. Walking by in the too-bright sunlight on his way to the liquor store, he saw that they had a HIRING sign in the window. He inquired within.

He took home a three-page application and laboriously filled it out, taking care not to drip scotch on the pages. There was no place on the application for his scholarly publications, his two published books, or his professional awards and recognitions. He thought it judicious to leave out the Ph.D in Philosophy from Princeton, the Rhodes scholarship, the postdoctoral work at the Heidelberg Institute in Germany, and the visiting professorship at Kings College, Oxford. He drew a line under his education at the B.A. he had earned at Yale and emended his major to business. He took the application back to the Radio Shack outlet on his next run to the liquor store.

Bingo! He was called in for an interview for a real job—in management. He had an irrational burst of joy when the telephone call came. The joy lasted a good few minutes, until the international operator called to tell him that his telephone number had been blocked at the number he'd been trying to reach in Spain; she was sorry.

Radio Shack's regional office was downtown in a small office building that the company shared with other electronics and tech companies' area headquarters. David found the Radio Shack office on the fourth floor opposite a company called Michauga Ltd. The Michauga sign was subtitled IDENTITY THEFT & DATA MINING SOFTWARE.

While sitting in the office of the overdressed yuppie Radio Shack executive—a black man in his early twenties—David tried to focus, but he kept thinking that he was in the wrong office, that he should be across the hall. Maybe there were people over there in Michauga Ltd. who could help him find his identity, which had been stolen in the night while he was sleeping. Maybe they could help him mine for a new, improved identity from somewhere deep on the Internet?

The Radio Shack executive was reciting his set piece about joining the Radio Shack team and getting on the Radio Shack wavelength. David registered about every third word. He tried pretending the young executive was one of his earnest grad students and did his active listening thing.

"I want you to tell me three personal qualities you have that would make you a successful Radio Shack manager," the executive said, articulating so carefully and exactly that David had the sudden flash that this young guy was bored out of his gourd with his job and doing anything to stay awake himself. He relaxed and talked to the guy.

*　　*　　*

David had scheduled a meeting with his attorney, Braxton Belyeu, at a downtown Austin bar, but not until after office hours. By the time Belyeu got there, David was slightly drunk. Belyeu came in, dark, baggy lawyer's suit, florid handpainted tie, and receding, slicked-back hair over a fleshy, somber face. Belyeu was a worst-case-scenario kind of lawyer, always leading with the cold facts and likely downside if he saw any possibility of one in the offing. If a client indicated he couldn't stand a bad outcome, he was no longer Belyeu's client.

He saw David's semiwasted condition the minute he sat down. He lost no time smacking him with the plain truth as he saw it. "Without successful completion of an alcohol treatment program," he said, "forget visitation. You'll be lucky if you get a Christmas card. And that's if there even *is* a custody hearing."

"What do you mean?" David said.

"If your wife can convince a Spanish court you're a danger to the child," the lawyer said, "you'll never see him again."

"He has to come back. He has to!" David said. Then he called to the passing waiter, "Hey, sir, can we have the same again here, please?"

The waiter approached. Belyeu put his hand over his glass. "I'm fine," he said.

David handed his empty glass to the waiter and turned back to Belyeu. "I'll just have to go and get him," he said.

"Europe ain't Mexico, David," Belyeu said. "They've got real borders. Maybe *you* can get in easy enough, but getting a six-year-old *out* is a whole different kettle of crawdads. You wanna see Jamie again? You get your life together. Pronto."

*   *   *

David Gale was a man who prided himself on
being in control of his life, a man who set substantial
goals, planned carefully thought-out attacks, and
went at his goals resolutely. That was how he had
got to his lofty position in his career. That was how
he had wooed and won his very attractive, pedigreed
wife seven years before. The booze was a diversion,
a little relief from the grind, a handy resource for
letting loose when he needed to. He could handle it;
he was always in control, never the booze. He
could've quit at any time, but why? Philosophers
since the Greeks had recognized that the pleasures
of wine could open a man's faculties to a full appreciation of the good, the true, and the beautiful.

The pleasures of wine, untempered by the Golden
Mean, could also send a man's life careening into a
black hole. So anguished was David over the separation from his beloved son that he was at the point
where he could either pour hemlock in his ear and
end the suffering, or take painful, dumb, conventional steps to try to play the game and get back the
key to the door.

Two nights later, in a low-ceilinged church base-
ment down by the river, he stood up in front of a
circle of Styrofoam cup–holding strangers. "Hi," he
said. "My name's David. I'm an alcoholic."

Smokers, most of them, they took puffs on their
sticks and watched him with practiced sympathy and
mild interest.

Constance's little bungalow, two blocks down from
Shoal Greek Green Belt, was freshly painted and
shined like a gem on a day of beautiful sunshine. It

would be several years before it would slide from this blessed state, become a locus of lurid curiosity, and fall into Goth Girl's care. Now it looked vastly different: flower beds, a well-manicured lawn, sparkling clean windows. The BLOCK HOME sign in the window was new.

David's Volvo pulled up in front. He parked and walked up to the front porch almost with a spring in his step.

Constance opened the door and saw David in a short-sleeved Radio Shack shirt and a tie. She was taken aback. She looked him over, bit her lip, and tried not to laugh. She searched for what to say and, at last, just gave a little shrug and said, "I'm sorry."

He pretended to be hurt, pretended not to understand why she wasn't digging his cool uniform. Then they both burst out laughing.

She hugged him as they laughed on the porch.

Constance's living room was Laura Ashley cozy. The sliding-glass door was open to the garden, so the room was sunny and breezy. Constance, leading David in, looked tired, but she was animated. She was animated enough for David to notice the behavior as something a bit different. Her hair too was different. Her face was a little drawn.

"You look good," Constance said, shifting the attention to him.

"I feel good," David said.

She smiled at him maternally, touched his face. They hugged again. "Welcome back," Constance said lightly, in his arms. "Look." She moved from him, took a photo from a case file on her table. "Betty Sue Johnson's been rescheduled," she said. "Her execution date's set for the fifteenth."

It was a photo of a young black woman. She had
a pleasant, timid demeanor. She certainly didn't look
like a murderer.

"I've got a conference call with Washington tonight," she said. "If the new national director will
commit emergency funds . . ."

She picked up a small plant as she moved toward
the porch.

David followed her, studying the photograph.
"Betty Sue will be commuted, and then you'll only
prove the system works," he said after some thought.

"But I'll save a life," Constance said.

He smiled at her, then noticed she had bruises on
her arms. "Where'd you get those?" David said.

She shrugged evasively. "Doing chores," she said.

"Your cowboy getting rough with you?" David
said, kidding.

She smiled at him sarcastically and mouthed *ha-ha*.

David watched as she walked through the arch-
way, self-consciously pulling down her sleeves. He
followed her as she moved onto the back porch and
down into the backyard.

Constance set down the plant among a dozen or so
others. "She was sentenced at seventeen," she said.

At the very back of the yard, the Cowboy worked
with a spade in a vegetable garden.

"Hey!" David said, calling to the Cowboy. "She
ever *not* make you work when you come by?"

" 'Mornin', David," the Cowboy said, raising his
spade in greeting. He was a serious-visaged, lean-
jawed, fortyish dude with slightly sad eyes. He
tipped his working gray Stetson back and gave
David a smile.

"So what's her story?" David said, turning to Constance with the picture he was still holding.

"I really want us to get behind this one," Constance said. "She's so articulate."

"Who did she kill?" David said.

"She'll put a face on the death penalty," Constance said.

"Constance?" David said.

Constance looked at him a beat, sighed.

"A cop," she said.

"You're crazy," David said simply, dropping the photograph to his side. "Not just your medium-grade, thinks-she's-Teddy-Roosevelt's-bathrobe, but stark-raving-loose-screws-in-the-belfry insane."

"Seventeen!" Constance said. "Four years before she could legally drink a beer!"

"You are a real danger to flora and fauna," David said.

"Are you gonna help?" Constance said.

"Of course," David said, with the smile.

He kissed her on the forehead. He drew back and looked at her. "You're burning up," he said.

She gave him a look. "I'm fine. It's a woman thing. Leave me alone."

He continued to watch her as she gathered her belongings to leave.

Chapter 18

David, wearing his Radio Shack shirt and carrying five large coffees on a tray, was happy as he walked out of the coffee shop into the warm night. He tried to sip one without spilling the others. A new life away from the University, a new start, sobriety—he actually felt better physically than he had in a long time. He sensed himself almost smiling.

As he walked toward the corner to cross the street, a red VW bug pulled up at the curb and a high school student jumped out the passenger side. She dashed past him toward the coffee shop. As David approached the VW, he saw that it was Denise, his former baby-sitter, sitting in the driver's seat. Their eyes met. He smiled. Denise smiled back, waved.

As he passed, he saw and heard the girl hit the car's automatic door-lock button.

The smile fell off his face. He kept going, crossed the street, walked on. The elusive split-second buzz of well-being was gone. These things were going to happen, he told himself. He tried to take it philo-sophically. He of all people should be able to do that, he thought wryly.

At the storefront marked DeathWatch, he turned around and backed through the door into the offices, balancing his coffees. It was the one steadfast point in his much altered life, this volunteer civic group. It was a touchstone for him and a reassurance, his codirectorship with Constance, and he was grateful for it. Going practically overnight from being lionized to being a leper was dizzying. Here he felt some balance return.

He entered the storefront carrying the coffees. Rosie sat at a desk, licking envelopes. Josh was on the floor beneath a desk, rewiring a computer terminal for Beth.

"Howdy, David," Josh said, calling from beneath the desk. He was trying to decode a ganglia of cables without laboriously untangling the whole mess.

"Hello, folks," David said. He went to Rosie, gave her a cup of coffee and three Sweet 'N Lows.

"Hello," Rosie said. "My, this *is* service. Thank you."

"Gladly," David said. He took one of the unsealed envelopes from her stack, then put a cup beside the legs of Josh. "Latte on your left, partner," he said.

Josh gave Rosie a look—they were surprised, pleased.

David made his way toward the back office.

"She's on the phone to Washington," Josh called.

"Mr. Sinclair," Rosie said helpfully. "The new national director."

The back office was as spartan as the rest of Death-Watch. File boxes were piled everywhere. Clipboard lists hung on the wall. Air-conditioning amounted to a window opened out to the alley behind.

David peeked in the door.

Constance waved him in. She sat at a desk talking on the speaker phone with DeathWatch National Director John Sinclair. Her slim hands and wrists framing the phone on the desk looked especially thin to David as he walked in.

". . . and see what kind of resources the religious groups can offer," said the voice of the DeathWatch head honcho from the speaker. The sporadic cacophony of a social gathering crackled in the background.

"I'm sure we can get some pulpit time," Constance said to Sinclair, "maybe cable."

David set her coffee down on the desk in front of her and took a seat off to the side.

"Cable's good," Sinclair said. "Listen, I need to run. For now, I agree, the first press release should focus on the woman's youth."

David clownishly held up the envelope for Constance to see, animatedly stuffed a flyer in it and licked and sealed it, then literally patted himself on the back. He grinned. Constance gave him an aren't-you-funny grin back, shaking her head.

"I'll have the Washington people look into counsel competency," Sinclair said, "though I'm almost sure she's exhausted this on appeal."

"John," she said, "David's going to—"

"Oh, I almost forgot," the DeathWatch director interrupted her. "Gale's not around, is he?"

Constance hesitated, looked at David. He shook his head no.

"No," Constance said.

"Good, keep it that away," the DeathWatch director said. "His relationship with DeathWatch is *over*. Last thing we need is this rape thing coming back to bite us on the butt."

Constance opened her mouth to say something, not sure how to react.

David just stared at her, stunned.

"And these guys don't stay on the wagon for very long, you know," the DeathWatch director added.

David stood up and left the room quickly. His coffee spilled. Constance could only watch.

"I'm serious, Constance. *Ban him from the premises.* I realize that the two of you . . ."

Constance ran around the desk, ignoring the voice on the phone, and raced after David.

By the time she hurried through the DeathWatch front office and got out onto the street and looked around anxiously, David was gone. She caught sight of his Volvo pulling out of a parking place and driving off down the empty main street. She stood watching him take the corner fast and disappear. She held her side and breathed deeply, a sense of doom descending on her.

At an ill-lit strip mall on a seedy south-side Austin street, David spotted a pay phone and pulled in. He parked the Volvo at an angle, lunged out, and grabbed the receiver. He punched in credit card numbers, home numbers, country code numbers, and a residence number in Spain. He was in a nervous panic. He looked across the street. There, staring him in the face, was a liquor store. David listened to a Spanish answering machine greeting.

"Sharon, pick up," David said into the phone. "I'm begging you. He's my son! Please! Please." He started to remove the phone from his ear.

"Hello?" Jamie said, his voice as clear as a crosstown call.

"Jamie?" David said, his heart pounding. "Is that you? It's Daddy. Jamie?"

"Mommy!" Jamie said, away from the receiver. "It's him. I didn't say anything, like you told me to . . ."

A click ended the connection. David listened to the sound of his own labored breathing in the receiver. Then a dial tone. He started slamming the receiver against the phone's body; he smashed it long after there was anything left to destroy, long after his hand bled.

He marched with purpose toward the liquor store, leaving the Volvo running, driver's door standing open. He strode across the street, daring the traffic to hit him.

Wearing a bathrobe, Constance walked out her front door at midmorning and went down the walk to the mailbox. She pulled out the mail and the *Austin American* and walked back toward her front porch, reading the front page of the paper. She looked tired, as though she hadn't slept in weeks. She climbed the porch steps and was about to pull the door open and go inside when she noticed a figure sitting in the corner of the porch. It was David, holding Cloud Dog. Unshaven, he wore his blue-and-white Yale sweatshirt. He had his Radio Shack shirt wrapped around his injured hand.

"You scared me," Constance said, startled.

"My sheep needs a manager . . . manger," David said, drunk to the gills.

"Are you okay?" Constance said. Stupid question. She could see he was a mess.

"Yes," David said. "No. I fell off a wagon."

"Come on," Constance said. "Come inside." She held the door open as he stood—she was too drained herself to help him. He stumbled inside.

"Know why Saint Jude is the patron saint of lost causes?" David said as they crossed into Constance's warm, cozy living room. He didn't wait for anyone else to answer. " 'Cause his real name was Judas," he said. He rambled around the room, coming to an unsteady stop and leaning against the back of the couch, holding the stuffed sheep. "There were two Judases—Judai, the saint guy, and the bad Judas, who ratted on Jesus *and* tried to kiss him. In medieval times they wouldn't pray to *good* Judas for fear of getting *bad* Judas on the line by mistake. Ergo, they only gave him business when really desperate. That's why. Then they changed his name."

Constance hadn't come into the room.

"Constance?" David said. He looked back toward the entry hall. The front door was still open. A small flyer lightly blew along the floor into the living room. "Your mail's blowing," David said. No answer. Where'd she go? He went and looked into the entry hall.

Constance lay unconscious on the floor near the open front door. The mail was scattered about her.

Chapter 19

The institutional fluorescents flew by overhead, making David dizzy, as he hurried along the hospital emergency room hallway trying to keep up with Constance. She was being wheeled on a gurney at code-blue speed by three ER staff members. Sobered up somewhat by fear, David grabbed the sleeve of one of the interns. "Will she be okay?" he said. "What is it? What?"

"Wait here," the ER staff member said, extricating his sleeve from David's grasp. He could smell the alcohol.

"I want to stay with her," David said.

"Wait here!" the ER staff member said, as though speaking to a child or a drunk.

"I can . . ." David said.

A burly orderly grabbed David and restrained him. "Hold up, Professor," the burly orderly said.

"I can . . ." David said, struggling to free himself.

"You wanna get arrested again?" the burly dude said in a fierce whisper.

David stopped struggling, dumbfounded. "How . . . do you know me?" David said.

"I watch the news," the burly orderly said, with a *duh!* look. "Now go wait." He released his bear hug.

David, his face full of confusion, stood staring after Constance on the receding gurney; then he turned away and moved slowly down the hall.

He passed out in a chair in the waiting room and slept it off. A stack of vending machine coffee cups on the floor beside him testified to his attempt to get straight before he zonked out. The hospital intercom calling doctors and announcing different codes didn't come close to penetrating his sleep.

A young female doctor sat beside him and lightly shook his shoulder. The second time she nudged him a bit harder. He woke, groggy.

"How we doing?" the doctor said without smiling.

"Fine," David said. "How's Constance?"

"Sleeping," the doctor said.

David collected himself and sat up as the doctor continued.

"Mr. Gale, a leukemia patient's condition is highly susceptible to external stress," she said. "While we don't want to totally restrict Constance's life—"

"What?" David said.

"Constance's illness requires a degree of regularity," the doctor said. She saw the look on David's face and stopped. A moment of silence ensued as the situation clarified for both of them. David was stunned, the doctor embarrassed. "You didn't know?" she said.

"No, no, I didn't," David said.

They sat in silence.

The disembodied voice over the hospital intercom piped, "Gale, time's up . . ."

*   *   *

What does that mean? thought Bitsey. Why, in the hospital waiting room, are they . . . ?

She snapped out of it. She was hearing the voice of the supervising guard speaking through the prison intercom. "Gale," the guard repeated, "that's all the time." Bitsey looked around.

David leaned back and took a long breath. He was in an emotional state.

Bitsey stared at him. Then, looking down at her pad, she realized she hadn't been writing on it for some time. She was amazed at herself, at the degree of her involvement.

"Funny how selfish we can be," David said. "When I heard Constance was dying, I was angry at her. I remember thinking, 'She knows how hard it is for me to need people.'" He stood, a sad smile on his face, and went to the back wall to be handcuffed.

"Why hadn't she told you?" Bitsey said.

"She said she was too busy," David said. "I guess she figured as long as death was chasing her, she could help others escape it. Constance left the world better than she found it."

He looked at Bitsey for a beat, but he was looking way beyond her. "It's a small, difficult thing," he said.

He turned without ceremony and left.

Bitsey sat there a few minutes unmoving, gathering herself.

The Ellis Unit parking lot had a good view of the exercise pens. Zack stood smoking, uneasily watching the cons working out, ropey masses of hyper-developed slow-twitch muscles from neck to ankles. Bulked-up man-weapons. Angry ones. Bored, depressed, claustrophobic, frustrated. He could not help envisioning those dudes walking free, catching up with him on a street outside the prison. They'd look at his skinny frame, squeeze him out both ends like an overripe banana, and toss him in a storm drain. He could feel a gigantic hand constricting his chest—when a real hand grabbed his shoulder.

"Fuck!" he said, badly spooked.

"Let's go," Bitsey said. She walked off toward their rental car. She was feeling weird, she thought to herself—kind of heavyhearted. What was the deal? Was she losing her edge? This was no time to get all human, she carped at herself. Snap out of it.

"Talked to the Austin prosecutor," Zack said. "Belyeu's a joke. Actually, the exact phrase he used was: 'Big hat, no cattle.' He was sanctioned twice and seriously fucked up the penalty phase. Gale could have gotten life on mitigating factors."

Bitsey was only half listening. But Zack's next remark penetrated her funk.

"Despite major pro bono offers from some of the top lawyers in the country," Zack said, "Gale stuck with him all through the appeals process. Which, by the way, Belyeu continued to screw up."

That rang a bell with Bitsey's earlier impressions of the case. She had thought it strange at the time that his original trial did not end up making anywhere near so big a splash as everyone had predicted. It was at least partly because he had turned down the big guns; he had not assembled a dream team. He had just the one attorney representing him, no showboating lawyers standing on the courthouse steps loudly impugning the prosecution, rousing public opinion. The trial had just kind of fizzled out.

And the appeals came and went without any hype whatsoever.

Why had Gale gone that route—the one-lawyer defense? Why had he rejected a more high-powered approach? She didn't know the answers to those questions, but his choice of tactics somehow fit with what she was piecing together about his psychology. There was something quite cool and self-possessed about the man, a refusal to be stampeded, even in these extreme circumstances. It was as though he was standing outside himself, observing and rather thoughtfully telling the story of what was happening to a third person. And Bitsey didn't get it. It didn't make sense to her. What was she missing about this guy? She had an uneasy feeling she was not seeing the big picture.

"What else?" Bitsey said.

"Nada on Berlin," Zack said, ticking off the highlights of his day. "We pick up the payola money in Houston tonight, overheat light came on twice, and you're not gonna believe what's going on in Huntsville."

Chapter 20

Protestors had begun to gather around the prison, specifically around the Huntsville Unit, which contained the Death House where the execution would take place. Police cars and barricades now blocked access to the entrance building and Welcome House. A few news trucks were already positioned near the press area, their big satellite uplink masts telescoped up for test transmissions.

The rental car moved through the morass of media squatters and their camps lined up along the side street skirting the Huntsville Unit. Strange, thought Bitsey, that the media army was already bigger for the death than for the defense. Or maybe not so strange, maybe entirely predictable. Since society's beginnings, public trials brought out the interested, the aficionados; public slayings brought out the blood-hungry hordes.

The rental car turned onto the street fronting the prison, and Bitsey and Zack drove slowly past the diverse and opposing protesting groups. Signs and banners identified a grab bag of points of view: law and order shouters and human rights pleaders, victims' rights advocates, constitutional lawyers, religious activists, defenders of juveniles and the retarded, international anti-torture-and-violence crusaders.

"What a life, waiting around for someone to die," Bitsey said.

"They won't even transfer him from Ellis until Friday," Zack said. He mimicked, " 'Let's go early, hon. We can watch 'em gas up the transport van.' "

Bitsey did a quick visual survey. A majority of the protesters so far were abolitionists. Amnesty International reps clustered beneath tarps. Catholic nuns sang hymns. There were food stations, sign-painting stations (DON'T KILL WITH MY TAXES! MARK 6:10, MURDER DOESN'T STOP MURDER!). Beneath one umbrella a large black woman sold candles.

Behind the Hang 'Em High barricade, a smaller contingent of pro–death penalty demonstrators had gathered, not yet a quorum, but one was expected. This was Texas, after all. A long-haired guy prepared signs while he listened to loud Southern rock: RAPE AND SUFFOCATE HIM! LET'S ROCK AND ROLL. A fundamentalist group had a blackboard with an hour-by-hour countdown. A big-chested, bearded dude wore a T-shirt that said, HEY, GALE, THIS BUD'S FOR YOU. He was selling little bottles of home brew called Lethal Injection.

TV crews were busy prerecording these and other vignettes, the whole panoply of "for" and "against" opinions, to use later with stand-ups.

A sudden burst of cheering and applauding from a knot of "againsts" drew Bitsey's and Zack's attention.

Demonstrators raised newly lettered signs calling

on President Bush to halt all executions. U.S. DISTRICT COURT JUDGE RAKOFF RULES DEATH PENALTY VIOLATES THE CONSTITUTION! announced one of the signs.

It was fabulous new ammo from a highly placed authority, crowed a young female antiexecutionist to a CNN reporter, displaying for the camera a copy of Rakoff's just-released district court decision. "Twelve death row inmates were cleared through ground-breaking DNA testing within the last year," the activist said. "The U.S. Supreme Court is on record saying, 'It is highly unlikely an executed person would subsequently be discovered to be innocent.' Judge Rakoff says, in so many words, 'Bull roar!' "

"Fuck, look," Zack said in amazement. "There's our friend."

They passed the Cowboy's pickup truck. Same gray Stetson, same lean jaw and sad dark eyes. He saw them and his expression changed to an odd smile. He touched his hat as they passed.

"This is getting a little too coincidental," Bitsey said.

The grizzled veteran reporter in Bitsey had been on the alert for some time. They were being watched, it was plain. They had been watched since before they hit town. She was trying to figure out why. Somebody must be nervous about what she and Zack might uncover. Who? Whose interests were served by ensuring that Gale went quietly to his grave without any further ado? Conversely, who would stand to gain if Bitsey somehow delayed or in fact derailed the process? She had come up with no answers to either question.

The Cowboy probably had some answers; that was a reasonable assumption, she thought. But did she have any real grounds for accosting him and demanding to know what the hell he was up to? She had nothing that would prevent him from calling her a crazy broad and giving her the bird. He was just an ordinary Texas guy sitting in his pickup truck in his own town, minding his own business. What was her problem?

The rental car drove slowly on past the gathering circus.

Interstate 45 was a 250-mile north-south speedway between Dallas and Houston. About three quarters of the way down to Houston, it skimmed past Huntsville, and the only cars likely to get off there were breakdowns, prisoner relatives, and curiosity seekers. The cars getting back on the interstate at that on-ramp were those who'd had enough voyeurism and/or prison visiting, folks with business to do in the big towns north and south, and occasional escapees. Bitsey and Zack had business to transact in the big town to the south.

They drove south and into Houston as far as the north loop of 610, the circumferential highway, and headed west along it. They got off near the chichi River Oaks section and followed Zack's handwritten directions along a broad boulevard to a nice upscale office park. At about ten to eight in the evening, they pulled in the empty parking lot, opposite a modern low-rise office building, and parked. They waited.

Within ten minutes, a black BMW pulled into the same parking lot, drove up, and parked next to them. John Barnes—the graying, Hobbitlike, and now grumpy bureau chief of the Houston bureau of *NEWS Magazine*—got out. He was a transplanted

Brit, and when dinner hour started for him, he didn't like its being interrupted until after he'd had his brandy *pousse-café*.

He popped the trunk of the BMW from inside, got out, and walked around to greet Bitsey. "Hello, dear," he said with a slightly waspish smile, kissing her cheek. "Wretched to meet under these circumstances— nothing like our Paris encounter."

"Hello, John," Bitsey said. "Good line, but we never had a Paris encounter."

"Oh, well," he said, "at least this time I can say that it was money that came between us." He pulled an aluminum suitcase from the trunk and presented it with a gentlemanly flourish.

Bitsey laughed. She'd walked straight into it. It would have been too much to expect an old-pro newsman like Barnes not to set himself up for a good juicy line in such a situation, one he could now embellish and tell over cocktails.

The transfer was made. Without fanfare or official procedures or armed guards. This was not after all something they as journalists did every day, or ever had before, for that matter. Barnes did, however, ask Bitsey to sign a release for the suitcase, and even that bit of officialese surprised her.

Deep Pocket, Zack took to calling him on the ride back, the man who kept a slush fund of a half million dollars in his car trunk in case a good story ever came his way after banking hours.

For Bitsey, this money thing was just another questionable aspect to a story she was feeling more ambivalent about every hour. Most irksome was the nagging sense she had that it was leading somewhere unpredictable. That, to a storyteller, should have afforded her nothing but delight. For some reason, it didn't.

Car headlights whooshed by on the interstate in front of the Huntsville Motel. Of the few cars that pulled off on the Huntsville exit ramp, none made the hard right turn and pulled in at the motel parking lot.

A pair of headlights flicked on in the parking lot, however—in one of the parking slots in front of Units 46 and 47. The vehicle backed up, swung around, and glided out into the street. The headlights turned not toward town, but instead went left and disappeared in the opposite direction.

It was another hour before a pair of lights pulled off Interstate 45 at the Huntsville exit and turned in the driveway of the motel. The car circled and pulled into a parking space in front of Units 46 and 47.

Bitsey and Zack got out. Zack was carrying the aluminum suitcase in his arms, clutched tightly.

"Relax, Zack," Bitsey said.

"It's a lot of money," Zack hissed.

They walked up a ramp to the second floor and along the walkway past other rooms. They turned a corner and came to Zack's door.

With a bluff, solicitous tone, Zack said to Bitsey, "So you coming in?"

"Excuse me?" Bitsey said.

"You wanna come in?" Zack said, not so confident.

Bitsey realized that he wasn't talking about journalistic research. She looked at him with disdain. "Please," Bitsey said.

Ready with his face-saver, he held up the suitcase and grinned. "I thought you were into guys with money."

She gave him the finger and walked away. God save me from testosteroney boys, she said to herself.

He chuckled and took out his key. Okay, so I'm no John Barnes with the suave one-liners, he thought. Not yet, anyway. I'll make her laugh somehow. He fiddled with the lock for a second, the metal suitcase snug between his knees.

"Zack!" Bitsey said.

Zack grabbed the suitcase from between his legs and ran to where Bitsey stood, still outside her room, staring at the door.

"What?" Zack said.

"It's open," she said.

"Maybe the maid forgot," Zack said.

"Look!" Bitsey said, pointing.

As he came to her door, he saw what had spooked her. Between the door and its frame, someone had stuck a roll of duct tape. It was holding the door ajar. "We gotta call someone," he said.

"Stand back," she said.

"Wait," Zack said.

It was too late. Bitsey pushed the door open. She saw something in the center of the room and entered.

Zack followed and saw what she saw. He set the aluminum case down on a table near the door. The fake oak nightstand that had stood against the wall between the two beds had been moved to the center of the room. On it was a lamp, turned on. Suspended just above the lamp, a VHS cassette hung from the ceiling fixture by a length of fishing line.

Subtle, thought Bitsey. Coulda missed that.

"Okay," Zack said. "This is fucked up."

"I'll check the bathroom," Bitsey said.

"I'm thinking that's a lousy idea," Zack said, ready

to bolt out the door at any sign of movement from the bathroom. Or closet.

Bitsey moved carefully through the room, checking the space between the beds, between the far bed and wall. She checked the coat closet. Finally, she approached the bathroom.

Anxiously, she pushed the door back and peered in. She reached in and flipped on the light. Nothing. The room seemed empty. She had no choice but to approach the shower curtain. Steeling herself, she pulled it back to reveal . . . an empty shower.

"Bitsey!" Zack said.

Bitsey came back into the main room to see Zack holding the VHS cassette. He had pulled it down from the ceiling, with the string still on it.

"Zack!" Bitsey said. "There could have been prints."

"Look," Zack said. He held up the cassette.

As she approached, she saw it was an ordinary cassette with a regular stick-on label. On the label had been typed, with an old typewriter, FOR BITSEY BLOOM.

Chapter 21

He had to convince them he knew how to wire it back up to the TV again. That, his driver's license left as security, and a twenty-dollar bill got Zack the loan of the reception office VCR. He ran out the motel office front door carrying the machine, the cables dragging on the ground behind him. He ran around and up the ramp toward the rooms.

Bitsey unlocked the door and let Zack in.

"The lady at the reception says no one asked for you," Zack said. "And all the room keys are different." He went to the TV. "Just she and her husband have masters," Zack said.

"What did you tell her?" Bitsey said.

"That you have a jealous boyfriend," Zack said. He started to hook up the VCR.

"Thanks," Bitsey said, irritated. "How about the VCR?"

"She didn't ask," Zack said. "I think she assumed it had something to do with why he was jealous. You sure we shouldn't call the cops?"

"Whoever got in here—without a key in broad daylight—was probably smart enough not to leave prints," Bitsey said. "I have the remote." She turned on the TV.

"Maybe they could look for DNA," Zack said. "Try 3."

"They don't look for DNA when someone breaks in to *deliver*, Zack," Bitsey said. "Here." She handed him the tape.

He started to put it in the VCR, hesitated, looked back at her. "You sure you want to see what's on here?" Zack said.

"No, but start it anyway," Bitsey said.

He put it in and pushed PLAY. She sat on the bed. He sat beside her. They watched a black screen for a moment.

"I hope this isn't what I think it is," Zack said.

They watched closely.

An image flickered in. It was a woman lying naked on a kitchen floor, facing away from the camera. An opaque white kitchen bag was over her head, sealed at the neck with duct tape. Her hands were handcuffed behind her. She was unmoving. She appeared dead.

"God, no," Bitsey said. She half turned away and turned back.

"Fuck," Zack said. "Is it her?"

"Turn it up," Bitsey said as they stared at the screen. She bit a thumbnail.

Zack turned up the sound. The audio was full of atmospheric hum. A refrigerator contributed its steady white noise. Birds could barely be heard in the distance. So could what sounded like a lawn mower—unnervingly normal background noises for a scene of confounding horror.

On the video, the woman lying in Constance's

kitchen did not move. Bitsey studied the surroundings. The kitchen was the same kitchen they had visited that morning in Austin under the care of Goth
Girl. It was cleaner than during their visit, Bitsey
noted, but otherwise unchanged. The kitchen gloves
that Zack had handled could be seen, lying upside-
down and rolled inside-out, on the dish rack beside
the sink. Near the body on the floor was a roll of
duct tape. In the lower-right corner of the screen was
part of what looked like a towel. Goth Girl had indeed said that a tripod for a video camera had been
found set up in the kitchen and that the killer had
probably videotaped his crime, but no tape had been
found. This was the tape.

Bitsey and Zack both jumped.

The static scene suddenly came alive.

A muffled sound came from the inert woman—she
seemed to return from death. Her wrists started to
pull against the handcuffs, then jerked at them. She
was alive, and panicked. Her legs flailed, kicking
against the counter. She screamed, the muffled and
frantic cries coming through the plastic bag. She
rolled onto her stomach; her whole body fought
against the locked handcuffs. She desperately rubbed
her face along the linoleum, trying to tear the plastic
bag that was now sucked in tight against her face,
suffocating her.

Bitsey, horror-struck, had to look away; then she
forced herself to keep watching. The woman's fren-
zied struggling went on for what seemed an eternity.
No help came. Then very quickly her energy began
to wane, and she jerked less. Her covered face now
turned toward the camera. Her head seemed to rock,
a sleepy nod. She seemed to be giving up. Her body

went slack. After several long, eerily still moments, the tape went black and staticky.

Zack and Bitsey sat there staring at the screen, blank tape scrolling past. Their skin was crawling; both were sweating, both incapable of words. What they had just sat through was a murder, the moment of a woman's death by violence. A snuff tape. It was something not remotely close to anything either of them had witnessed before. They heard themselves praying, in their different ways, never to see anything like it again. They were sick and frightened.

Bitsey waited outside on the motel gangway, pulling in breaths of the cool night air. She stood at the railing, looking out at a thunderstorm gathering on the horizon. Her head in a turmoil, she was re-sorting her view of herself as a tough-minded, thick-skinned grown-up who had seen everything and could handle anything. She was compulsively replaying the tape's sounds and images in her mind. She sensed they were there permanently; she would be replaying them forever.

The phone banged down inside, and Zack came out and stood beside her. "Belyeu says to bring the tape first thing tomorrow," he said, exhaling, trying to relax. "He also said you were right about not calling the police."

She kept looking straight ahead at the distant boiling storm clouds.

"Are you gonna be okay?" Zack said.

Bitsey took a deep breath, turned to him, held his eyes. She shook her head no. Her lips started to tremble and her eyes brimmed uncontrollably. He put his arms around her as she started to cry.

*   *   *

They picked at their steerburgers and coleslaw in a busy Huntsville sports bar, a spot they chose for the amount of protective if heedless humanity per square foot. Whoever planted the tape in Bitsey's room was surely still watching them and could probably mess with them in whatever venal way he chose. Why make it easy for him?

From their booth, Bitsey and Zack watched an out-of-town TV crew set up and interview a pair of local college kids standing at the bar.

"Never heard of him," said a buzz-cut dude wearing a HOOK 'EM HORNS sweatshirt. "There's a lot of executions these days."

"Me either," the girl said. "He deserves it, though." She sipped her drink thoughtfully. "Probably," she added.

Zack's reaction was to scoff at the kids' ignorance.

Bitsey's reaction was different, and it surprised her a little. Having just seen the brutal murder of a fellow human being, she found herself unwilling to contemplate any more killing, even the killing of a killer. She had never had a single strong opinion about capital punishment: an abused ghetto kid who'd never had a break—let him rot in prison; a John Wayne Gacy/gruesome serial killer—let him fry.

But now she listened to the clueless college kids and she wanted to spare them the horror; she wanted them to care enough not to kill or be killed. She wanted—God knows where it was coming from—to save them. She took a big hit on her drink, hoping to stun her brain back into working order.

Zack smoked. The VHS cassette sat on the table between them, as did a small stack of Bitsey's crumpled tissues. She couldn't stop sniffling.

The waitress stopped at their table and refilled their coffee cups.

They waited until she left and then whispered intensely. "Let's say Gale's telling the truth," Zack said. "Maybe some right-wing fuck set him up, arranged a perfect murder. Why send a magazine journalist proof a few hours before he's won? Doesn't make sense."

"No, it's perfect," Bitsey said. "He knows how hard it is to get a retrial in Texas. He knows the magazine can't give this any substantial play before the execution—we'd have to give it to a daily or a network and that won't happen. But mostly he knows I'll tell Gale tomorrow."

"So?" Zack said.

"What if Constance's murder was just a means of getting at Gale?" Bitsey said. "Not only to get rid of him, but to make abolitionists look crazy. 'Of course he sympathizes with murderers—he is one.' You make sure he sits six years on death row for a brutal rape and murder. Then you let him die—die knowing everyone will remember him with disgust. You destroy his life, his work, his memory—and then you make him watch."

"That's a lot of hate," Zack said.

Bitsey gestured to the VHS cassette and made a need-I-say-more face.

"Then why release it?" Zack said.

"It's no fun if you keep it to yourself," Bitsey said. She scooped up the tape.

The storm hit about two a.m. It was one of those heavy summer thunderheads that collects its dark force out over the Gulf of Mexico and assaults the

Texas lowlands from the Louisiana border to the Rio Grande. This one rolled in over the intercoastal waterway between Port Arthur and Galveston and marched on a broad front up the Trinity River Basin and over the Sam Houston National Forest toward Huntsville. It battered the town and its high-walled prisons, striking with lightning and earsplitting thunder cracks that dissipated in lingering rumbles like the tail ends of ferocious arguments.

A figure stood at a dark window of the Huntsville Motel, looking out. A line of lightning cracked the sky in two. The strobing light picked out Bitsey, intently watching the night and the tumult. She couldn't sleep; she could only churn. And tear up and sob over the incessantly looping images of Constance Harraway dying in agony. The storm felt God-awful apt to her—nature roaring that something sick and out of balance was afoot, that other irretrievable human acts were in the offing.

Chapter 22

On the road again, the rental car kept up a steady speed westward, traveling the maddeningly indirect series of two-lanes toward Austin. It was Thursday morning and still gray and pelting down rain.

Bitsey, driving on very little sleep, found herself slipping again and again into a memory trance and had to jerk herself out of it. It was their third day in Texas, and it felt to her like their third month. The emotional topography in the hard, flat state was jagged and punishing.

Zack checked the backseat; the aluminum suitcase and an umbrella sat on it.

Bitsey checked the overheat light on the dash as she drove. It was not on steadily but flickered on and off annoyingly. They had checked the coolant a dozen times. The coolant was fine.

"Why do they call it checkbook journalism if we pay cash?" Zack said. He looked out the back window. "Whoa, we got company," Zack said.

"The Cowboy?" Bitsey said.

They could see the pickup through the tire mist fifty yards behind them. "Yeah, and doing a lousy job of hiding," Zack said.

Bitsey kept glancing in the rearview mirror, Zack out the back window.

"He must think we're idiots," Zack said.

Bitsey didn't repond, just watched in the mirror. "Is he gaining?"

"No," Zack said. "Just sitting back there."

"Can you see the license plate number?" Bitsey said.

"Too much mist," Zack said.

They kept glancing back. The pickup stayed right there in the rearview mirror, never more than ten or twelve car lengths behind.

"What the fuck does this guy want?" Zack said.

The money in the aluminum case in the backseat suddenly became the elephant in the room you were not supposed to think about. Bitsey and Zack both chose not to bring it up. They were dragging around a small fortune and had no protection, no defense, if attacked. What had they been thinking? They'd been thinking that the hide-in-plain-sight technique was the way to go. They'd been thinking that if they carried out the money thing without any fanfare, drawing no attention to it, the chances of running into trouble were infinitesimally small. Who would know? Who would have any idea that two mooks like them would be muling half a mil?

Maybe somebody did know, and the Cowboy was in on it. Had they been blindly stupid?

Belyeu & Crane, Law Offices, was in a restored Colonial-style town house in downtown Austin. It wasn't F. Lee Bailey or Jerry Spence territory, with phalanxes of associates standing by and flashy high-heeled assistants running in with cappuccinos and Havana Havanas and calls from George Jr. at 1600.

It was a small set of disarmingly chaotic offices, and it did have a view of the rain-soaked capitol.

A thoughtful-looking black clerk, Aaron, sat at a corner table in Belyeu's office, counting the money from the aluminum suitcase, watching Bitsey out of the corner of his eye.

Bitsey waited on a huge sofa opposite the desk. She stared straight ahead, relieved to have the money off her hands. The Cowboy had tailed them all the way into Austin, but they had lost sight of him before they found 420 Congress Avenue and pulled into the Belyeu & Crane parking lot.

Braxton Belyeu appeared just outside his door, trailed by a young file clerk. "Fine," Belyeu said, as usual in his slightly baggy but expensive lawyer's suit. "Oh, and bring in Miss Bloom's original when that's done." He walked in past Bitsey. "Don't blame you for not watching that twice," he said with a rueful shake of the head. He moved behind the desk and started sifting through papers.

"I couldn't sleep afterward," Bitsey said.

"I understand," Belyeu said. "I generally tell folks I'm no more afraid of the Grim Reaper than I am of a Presbyterian on Mother's Day." He chuckled to himself, but not much. "But watching that tape . . . well, I had to keep tellin' myself, 'That's not Constance,' just to get through."

He let that thought hang there for a moment. "Unfortunately," he said, "others may argue the same."

"Yeah, but it's her kitchen, in her house," Bitsey said.

"Currently home to Weirdos, Incorporated," Belyeu said. "Arguably, that tape could have been made by anybody with twenty dollars and a tolerance for vulgarity."

"Will it get us a postponement?" Bitsey said.

"Us?" Belyeu said. He smiled.

Bitsey inwardly grimaced; she had said *us*.

"This ain't my first rodeo, Miss Bloom," Belyeu said. "I gotta tell you that there's a machine a-runnin'. And come six o'clock tomorrow night, that machine wants to be fed."

Bitsey tried to gauge Belyeu. He seemed more substantial here in his own inner sanctum than at the prison and he did not give off the air of the flake that Zack's report made him out to be. He seemed solid and knowing, not a posturing, empty suit. Not the fool who had blown David Gale's defense. Well, she'd been fooled before.

Aaron put the last of the money back into the suitcase. "All here, Mr. Belyeu," he said.

"Thank you, Aaron," Belyeu said. As Aaron got up and moved to the door, nodding to Bitsey as he went, Belyeu walked out from behind his desk. "To add to our troubles," he said to Bitsey, "your own credibility might come into question."

Bitsey allowed Aaron to depart before responding. "Why?" she said.

"You've been fraternizin' with the condemned," Belyeu said. "In the court's eyes, he's the most likely candidate to have put you on to the tape. He's a persuasive man, you're an out-of-state woman—it don't look good."

"But someone put the tape in my room!" Bitsey said.

"A fact for which we have no evidence," Belyeu said.

A very professional-looking Latina assistant, Bobbi, entered and handed Bitsey her video.

"Thank you, Bobbi," Belyeu said.

"Thanks," Bitsey said, thinking again, This does not look like the crackpot organization Zack reported it to be. Everybody seemed to know what he or she was doing.

"Well, let's not throw a pity party and sit around readin' Kafka," Belyeu said, standing. "Could be we find a sympathetic judge. I'll file within the hour. You headin' back over to see Gale?"

"Yeah," Bitsey said, standing.

"Fine," Belyeu said. "I'll call over to the motel later and give you an update."

Bitsey considered him for one irritated moment. This is life-and-death stuff here, she wanted to say, how about showing a little excitement? She said nothing and left.

She rode down in the crowded elevator, lost in thought about her conflicting impressions of Belyeu. She couldn't read the man. There was a kind of detachment about his attitude toward Gale and his dire plight that could have been just emotional self-preservation on his part, professional detachment, or some other weird thing she couldn't fathom. Maybe it was just that silky duplicity that certain Southern men cultivated as the veneer of their superiority, which she despised. Whatever it was in Belyeu, it annoyed Bitsey. She was used to reading people handily, and when she couldn't, she bristled.

As she exited the elevator into the alcove on the ground floor, she saw a woman unsnap her umbrella and realized she'd forgotten hers in Belyeu's office. She turned back to the elevator door just as it closed. "Shit," she said. She stood debating for a few seconds, looked at her watch, and turned away from the elevators. She started out toward the main lobby, but when she did she saw the Cowboy sitting in a corner chair.

The lean-faced man, wearing the Stetson as always, was tilted forward watching the people Bitsey had been in the elevator with exit through the lobby. She, however, was later coming out than the others, several dozen yards behind them, and he didn't spot her before she saw him.

She froze and took several steps back into the alcove. She turned and headed in the other direction, out the back doors of the building.

She dashed across the Belyeu & Crane parking lot in the pouring rain to the rental car. Zack was half dozing in the passenger seat as she knocked on his window. He had to turn over the ignition so he could roll down his window—all the time she was standing out there getting soaked.

"Did you see the Cowboy?" Bitsey said, leaning down.

"He went in Belyeu's building?" Zack said.

"He's in the lobby," Bitsey said. "I need you to tail him. Get a license number. We have to find out who he is. Promise me you won't screw this up, Zack. It's important. Gale's life . . ." She couldn't, or wouldn't, finish.

Zack noted her change in attitude. "How are you gonna get to the prison?" Zack said.

"Taxi," Bitsey said, moving away, waving him to get to work.

Chapter 23

A few minutes late for their third and final scheduled interview, and still in her raincoat, Bitsey rushed in through the doors of the Ellis Unit visitation area to find Gale already sitting there waiting for her. Wet and hugging herself, she paced in front of him, explaining her day and the unsettling events of the night before.

"Okay, okay," David said. "Calm down."

Over the loudspeaker the disembodied voice of the supervising guard boomed, "Visitor needs to stay seated."

"Maybe you should sit down," David said.

She sat with a huff.

"His name is Dusty Wright," David said. "He was the local DeathWatch director before Constance. He was a 'bullhorner'—a zealot who thinks a good demonstration has to end in a riot and arrests. Death-Watch fired him for punching someone at a rally, but Constance kept him in the organization. He adored her. They were close. Real close. He testified at my trial."

"He testified to support you, or to oppose the death penalty?" Bitsey said.

"He testified against me," David said.

"Against you?" Bitsey said. Realizing they were into Gale's story, she scrambled to get out her reporter's notebook and start writing things down.

He nodded.

She stared at him a moment. The old silent response: as good as the best question.

His tone softened. This was a hard thing for David to address. "He testified about the drinking," he said. "Alcohol is a mitigating factor in capital cases. I . . . I always told myself it was his sick way of helping me get a reduced sentence."

He went quiet for a moment. "I suppose he really believes I killed her," David said. "Dusty's a man easily blinded by hatred."

Bitsey looked up at him with a flash of recognition.

Zack was driving like a teen goofball, running yellow lights, cutting in and out of lanes. But it was in the line of duty.

He was hot on Dusty's—the Cowboy's—trail. Keep calm, he told himself, but he was plenty pumped. It was all he could do not to run the rental car right up the tailgate of the pickup. This was his first car pursuit, ever. And it was officially sanctioned. This was what big-time journalism was all about, he thought exuberantly. This was why he'd turned down a better-paying job doing computer programming for a mapping company and had instead taken the entry-level job as intern/editorial assistant at *NEWS Magazine*. This was the big time.

Zack was no slug. He'd graduated well up in his class at Swarthmore, without appearing to be any more of a grind than the rest of the hypermotivated student body. He wrote stories and took photographs for the school paper his last two years and did a summer internship at his hometown newspaper. He got a Fulbright to teach in Turkey for a year, an experience that expanded his vision about the wider world enough to convince him he didn't want to just go back to America and commit his life to some corporation.

As was the fashion of the day among his fellow graduates, Zack yearned to do many things, not just one, for his life's work. He figured that, if he became a journalist and wrote about other people's lives, he'd get a taste of a thousand different career paths, and from among them, he could choose the ideal one—or several—for him. What he didn't know was that many, many journalists before him started out with that same frame of mind and found themselves forty years later still ink-stained wretches, still searching for their real and ideal life's work.

Zack gave no thought to what he'd do if the Cowboy stopped and came back to confront him. He just figured the guy didn't have a clue he was being tailed, since he'd never expect Bitsey and Zack to be behind *him*.

Through his windshield spattered with pouring rain, the wipers beating angrily, Zack watched the pickup glide through the traffic leaving Austin. The truck headed north up Texas 35, the main highway to Dallas–Fort Worth. It sped through Pflugerville and then took the bypass off the turnpike into Round Rock. There the Cowboy followed a circuitous route around the little downtown, plowing through the overflow from side-street storm drains. Zack cat-and-moused with the truck through the run-down burg and was still on its tail when it turned east and headed out of town on a county road.

Within a mile and a half they came to a flashing railway crossing with no barrier. The pickup decelerated as a slow-moving goods train approached, then suddenly accelerated and shot through the crossing. Zack hit the gas to do the same, then slammed on the brakes, demonstrating his innate intelligence and high-priced education at the last possible moment. He chickened out, brought the rental car to a stop, and watched the train go blasting through.

"Fuck," he said.

Dusty, eyeballing the clear road and the train sliding past in his rearview, smiled wanly and wheeled off onto the first ranch road to the north. He jumped over to Route 79 going east and headed back toward Huntsville.

In Ellis Unit visitation, Bitsey was seated across from David, leaning forward, eyes locked on his, bent on getting the whole story and in a hurry. Time was running out, she was keenly aware. And to her great surprise, she felt herself tightening up. What was that about? Bitsey Bloom, the seasoned pro, the old hand at working against the clock. She was the best in the house at getting the real story, getting it straight, getting the proper context, and above all getting it filed on time. She had never missed a deadline. She just notched it up a gear when she had to and got the job done. This was different. She was amazed.

"Maybe he hated you because you were seeing Constance," she said.

"I wasn't 'seeing' Constance," David said.

"She had your semen . . ." Bitsey said.

"It's more complicated than that," David said.

David Gale, no longer codirector of DeathWatch, moved around the edges of the crowd handing out leaflets to newcomers. Another abolitionist worked the other side of the growing gathering. The tired DeathWatch volunteers held signs with photos of Betty Sue Johnson.

Constance had scheduled the protest at the state capitol in Austin for maximum exposure. She convened the rally at the base of the capitol steps in full view of the governor's office, with the stately building as the irresistible backdrop for TV stand-ups. Remote video crews of the three local Austin stations focused their cameras as Constance rose to speak on a raised dais.

A DeathWatch banner hung behind her. Dusty, Rosie, and Josh waited at one side of the podium. Two policemen on horseback sat bored on the mall. Uninterested newspaper and TV reporters stood behind the crowd.

David turned to watch.

Though Constance was frail and sickly, her voice had surprising strength. "When you kill someone, you rob their family," she said, "not just of a loved one, but of their humanity. You harden their hearts with hate. You take away their capacity for civilized dispassion. You condemn them to bloodlust."

She paused to cough, amid some dutiful applause.

"It's a cruel, horrible thing," she said. "But indulging that hate will never help. The damage is done, and once we've had our pound of flesh we're still hungry. We leave the Death House muttering that lethal injection was just too good for them. In the end, a civilized society must live with a hard truth. He who seeks revenge digs two graves."

Constance started to cough again and couldn't stop. "Excuse me," she said. "I . . ."

Pom! Pom!

Muffled gunshots echoed off the capitol facade. The policemen sat up in their saddles or stood up in their stirrups, looking hurriedly around.

It was Constance who had been hit. A sudden bright red spot grew on her blouse. She looked down, stunned and confused.

David ran forward and jumped onto the dais. By the time he reached her, she was staring at her bright red hand.

"It's okay. . . . I . . . I think . . ." Constance said.

He ripped open her blouse. The skin beneath was unbroken. She had been hit with two paintballs.

"It's paint," David said. The dull sound of the shots now made sense. It had been two short blasts of high-pressured air.

"There!" Josh said, pointing. "That's him!"

Amid the pandemonium of the crowd milling in all directions, a young man in a bandana started running as he put away his paintball gun. David leapt off the dais and ran after him. The young man saw he was running right at the mounted police and turned back, giving David an advantage.

David caught him by the collar and spun him around. The young man spat in his face. David raised his fist, hesitated . . .

"Go on," the young man said. "Go on."

David stared at him. In that moment of hesitation, the young man lunged and tried to wrench free. David held on and pinned his arms with a bear hug. Suddenly Dusty was there, flush with rage, punching the now-defenseless kid.

Once. Twice.

"What the fuck are you doing?" David said, trying

to spin the kid away. He was still holding the paintballer as Dusty grabbed him and hit him again. Blood exploded from the kid's mouth and covered his face.

David let go of the kid and grabbed Dusty to stop him from hitting the kid again.

"Stop!" David said. "Stop it!"

Dusty fought to free himself as the kid ran away.

"Goddamn you!" Dusty said.

"Don't you see?" David said. "That's just what they want!" He pointed to the news crews with their remote video cameras shooting this in full and from every angle. They'd taped the whole ugly scene.

In a fierce whisper, David flayed Dusty. "You're crazy!"

"And you're a coward," Dusty hissed.

Chapter 24

The TV video footage was damning. There was no getting away from it. All three local stations had it on their own tape, and they replayed it several times during each news segment.

David watched it standing in Constance's living room. Over and over on the screen, Dusty punched the young man in slow motion. The video made it look as though David was holding the kid so Dusty could punch him. It was hard to imagine, from the cuts shown, any other explanation. The voice-over commentary described a capital punishment protest that got out of hand, with strong feelings and violence on both sides, noting the irony of anti-execution protesters using personal violence to make their point.

The news program cut to file tape of David's debate with Governor Hardin, using a sound bite of David saying, "The old law of eye for an eye leaves us all blind."

The next cut was to Dusty's punch, again in slow motion. Then the report cut in a series of sound bites from previous coverage of David's speeches and news conferences, selecting his most passionately expressed views. The effect was a classic media lynching, distortion by selection, portraying David Gale as a seething heap of aggression just waiting to explode.

Constance had had enough. Frustrated, sick at heart, she turned off the television.

David stood behind her in silence, numbed by this strange turn. What could he say? When it didn't seem as though it could get any worse, it did. And in a new, excruciating way—a blow to their cause, their cherished crusade.

"By now every media outlet in the state has it," Constance said. She thought about it all. She finally turned to him. "And guess who will suffer?" she said, the weariness evident in every word.

Any hope that Betty Sue Johnson had of escaping execution through the good offices of DeathWatch was lost. Not a single one of the rally protesters' arguments in favor of commuting this woman's sentence to life made the news reports the night before. The governor did not even bother to make a pro forma statement about justice being done and society's interests being served.

The clock outside Betty Sue Johnson's cell in Ellis Unit ticked down without interruption. Her time to expire approached without any last flurry of dissent. She was transferred to Huntsville Unit at the designated hour. She said good-bye to her family, who had gathered in great number. The lethal injection chamber was made ready.

Betty Sue Johnson's photograph was prominently displayed by the protestors outside the Huntsville Unit. They chanted and sang and held a candlelight vigil, but without expectation of changing anyone's mind.

Over in the press area, seven print journalists but no TV crews, fanned themselves in the heat. They made no attempt to go among the protestors and elicit quotes; they were there in case something other than the standard functioning of the state human-disposal machine should take place. In case, that is, there was news. Another uneventful execution was not news—it would be the forty-third at Huntsville that year, the total approaching three hundred persons since the death penalty had been reinstated in Texas. Close to five hundred more waited their turn on death row out in Ellis Unit. They couldn't all be news.

Dusty the Cowboy stood directly behind the barricade watching the door of the Huntsville Unit, his lean, drawn face showing more anger than usual. He held his cell phone to his ear and looked at his pocket watch. The watch read 6:26.

The journalists seemed to come to attention as Duke Grover, head bearer of bad news, escorted five black witnesses out of the prison doors.

"They're bringing Betty Sue's people out," Dusty said into the cell phone.

The vigil was on at DeathWatch in Austin, as was their custom, but without even the faint flicker of hope that leavened other vigils.

The atmosphere was tense and oppressive. Josh watched his computer screen closely. Rosie waited at her desk fiddling with papers. Beth sat against the wall breaking up a Styrofoam coffee cup into tiny pieces.

In the center of the room, a middle-aged priest

quietly prayed while holding the hands of a large black woman, who murmured affirmations. Conspicuously absent from the little community was David Gale, one of its founding figures and moving forces. He was now a liability and a drag to the organization he had founded, and he had to stay away.

DeathWatch's in-house vigils for executions had no practical effect. The organization was a nerve center, it was true, in case of the last-minute surfacing of evidence or information that might lead to a stay. But in actuality, that never happened.

The vigils did have a point, however. They were public moral gestures, acts of solidarity with the about-to-die, statements that somebody was watching, somebody cared, somebody was working tirelessly and would go on working tirelessly to put an end to capital punishment. State-sponsored killings affected us all, the gesture said; you turn a blind eye to questionable acts of your government at peril to your own soul. It is the duty of citizens to bear witness, said the vigils. Nations that dim the lights and do their dirty work in darkened back rooms are judged harshly by history for it. Let us perform our acts of state in the bright light of public exposure. Let us be clear-eyed about what we do in the name of justice and retribution. Don't turn away and say you didn't know. Look. Know. Taste the awful finality, extremity, and moral weight of taking a human life. And decide anew each time if you want this to continue in your name.

Constance was on the phone, on the open line with Dusty. She took a moment to absorb the news.

"Thank you, Dusty," Constance said.

The room's occupants all exchanged glances.

Constance slowly hung up the phone. She weakly stood, walked to the wall of photos, and marked a red X through the photo of Betty Sue Johnson. Staring at the woman's image, she hugged herself, warming her thin bones against a sudden chill on this hot night. This one was hard for her to take. She was on the verge of tears as Rosie came up behind her.

"Look at these losers," Constance said. "Rednecks. Ghetto hustlers. Drug addicts. Schizophrenics. They're murderers. Who cares if they die?" She was breaking down.

Rosie tried to comfort her, rubbing her shoulder.

"Who cares if the cycle goes on?" Constance said. "Who cares . . . ? Who . . . ? Who . . . ?" Her tears erupted. Rosie took her in her arms and buried her friend's face in her shoulder.

Outside the DeathWatch office, on the sidewalk close by the front door, a beefy security guard moved back and forth. He kept watch up and down the block and eyeballed approaching cars—a response to the paintball attack at the rally. The guard kept checking his watch, aware of the execution schedule, aware this was a key time if pro–death penalty louts were going to attack or create an incident.

Rosie and Constance could be seen embracing through the storefront window, as Constance cried. Watching from across the street was David, who sat on the hood of his car. His travel cup rested on the hood.

In his hands was a child's drawing. He looked from Constance crying to the drawing. In the background of the drawing was Gaudi's church and a matador. Prominent in the foreground were three labeled figures: Sharon ("Mommy"), Jamie ("Me"),

and Guillermo ("Papa Guillermo"). David looked
back up at Constance and rocked slightly in pain
and impotence. He suddenly jumped off the hood,
slammed into the driver's seat, and wheeled away.

At his wit's end, Gale drove. He had to talk to
somebody. His colleague—once his good friend—
Ross would talk to him, but he was not at home.
David drove some more. And drank from his travel
cup. He looked at his watch: eight p.m. Ah! The famous Joyce seminar. Ross's claim to fame. He turned
onto the sprawling U.T. campus.

In Hamilton Hall, in a small, elegant conference
room with a mahogany table and leather captain's
chairs, Ross was conducting his popular undergraduate seminar. Bryan, the brightest star among the nine
students, was explaining that though he had steeped
himself in *Finnegan's Wake* and wallowed in the
music of the language, very little of its meaning had
penetrated his willing skull.

"Of course you don't understand Joyce," Ross said.
"He doesn't want to be understood, Omelia, my boy!
He wants to be remembered."

The door whipped open. Enter David in his shirtsleeves. Drunk. Very drunk. He stood there, travel
cup in hand, looking intense and quizzical. And
unsteady.

A couple of the students laughed at the timing: a
genuine Joycean moment, Buck Mulligan himself, in
his cups, looking for God's truth.

"Mr. Gale, can we help you?" Ross said to David.

"I . . . I . . . no," David said. He hesitated, seemed
to hear a voice screaming in his head. He frowned
at the lot of them, took a long look at the stranger
Ross, and exited.

Ross made an ah-a-visit-from-the-local-weirdo face. A few students chuckled.

David careened out of Hamilton Hall and caught his balance against a drinking fountain. As he had a thousand times before, he started down the tree-lined brick walkway that formed the backbone of the campus. But on this occasion he stumbled along, clearly in a drunken stupor. One of the most highly recognizable figures on campus, once revered, once celebrated, he now became the object of stares, mumbles, snickers. He went from oblivious one minute, Jamie's phone voice replaying in his head, to hyperaware the next, hearing everything. The students' voices reached him in loud whispers. Louder.

He fell to his knees in the center of the walkway.

Louder.

Mortified, he covered his ears against a symphony of contempt. A disgusted male student put his foot against the drunk's shoulder and shoved him out of the way.

Professor David Gale rolled over in a pitiable heap, staring up through tears at the blurry stars.

Chapter 25

Constance's back porch received the dishonored guest. He sat holding a cup of coffee, staring out at the backyard, breathing in the aroma of the blooming lantana and honeysuckle, gazing up at the night sky with somewhat clearer eyes. The stars were Texas close. He was listening on the phone as he watched the stars, hoping. A recording with a Spanish voice was talking. He had enough Spanish to know the voice was saying the number he had dialed was no longer in service. He let it repeat a couple of times.

Constance came through the open sliding-glass door wearing a turtleneck sweater and wrapped in an afghan, despite the balminess of the night. She looked up at the stars for a quiet minute. "Remember those Kübler-Ross stages, the ones the dying go through?" Constance said.

"Denial, anger, bargaining, depression, and acceptance," David said. "Where are you?"

She sat in a lawn chair beside him. "Denial," Constance said.

"Denial's my personal favorite," David said. They sat in silence, in perfect acceptance of denial under the quiet night sky.

"The whole idea of being a process makes me tired," Constance said. "I'm not up to the job of dying person. Marveling at the blades of grass. Lecturing strangers to relish every moment. "

"Mending bridges," David said.

"Mending bridges," Constance said. "Confessing regrets. Uuuggh."

"No regrets?" David said. He knew something about regrets. He seemed to know about little else, advanced degrees notwithstanding.

"Nope," Constance said. She stared off—a thoughtful moment. "Take that back," Constance said. "I wish I'd had a child."

"Me too," David said. Then regretted his comment. Me, me, me.

"I'm sorry, David," Constance said. She reached over and put her hand on his arm. "I guess I just wish I would have risked more," she said. "Oh, and not enough sex. Should have had more sex."

"How much . . . how many lovers have you had?" David said.

"Including college?" Constance said.

"Including college," David said.

Her hand, still on his arm, held up four fingers.

"Well, it's . . ." David said. "Not everybody . . . yeah, you should have had more sex."

She laughed, coughed. He laughed. Their laughter trailed off into the night. He took her hand in his.

"You work hard not to be seen as a sex object," Constance said. "Before long, you're not seen at all."

"I see you," David said. He saw a pretty woman with intelligent, sympathetic brown eyes and long, soft hair falling below her shoulders. He saw a warm and welcoming smile. He saw an alluring, feminine woman any man would want to hold. He did not see the sick Constance at all; he saw the healthy, feisty female he had known for many years.

They were holding hands in the air, their elbows on the chairs' armrests. "Want to make it five?" he said. "Finish the hand?"

"A pity lay?" Constance said. "No, thanks."

He thought about that. They watched their fingers lightly playing with one another. "It wouldn't be pity," David said.

They turned. Their eyes met and held.

Constance's bedroom was one place in her house David had never been. They had been many things to each other—friends, colleagues, sparring partners, confidants, lunch companions, running buddies, gossip sharers—but never lovers. Time changes lives and relationships. This was a change neither had foreseen. These were lives so altered that they were in some sense new.

The newness was what Constance and David felt most, in bed together, naked with each other for the first time, making love. He lay on top of her, covering her, one of his hands supporting her head, the other stroking her face. They kissed tenderly. It was less strange than they had feared, less awkward, more comforting. He started moving, gently.

"Are you okay?" he said.

She murmured. "Don't worry," she whispered.

He kissed her neck.

"It's good," she said, and smiled. "Talk to me. Let me hear your voice."

"I'm here," David said, moving up to her ear. "Happy. I'm very happy." He kissed her mouth, moved against her in delicate rhythm. Her moans took on a teary edge. Their voices, barely whispers, blended into one another.

"Hold me tight," she said.

"I'm here," David said.

"Tight . . . I'm scared," she whispered.

"It's okay," David said.

She had begun to cry.

He stopped moving, kissed her tears.

"Don't stop," Constance said. "Stay in me. Please stay in me."

He moved again, slowly. "Shh," he said. "I'm staying."

"I need to feel you inside."

He could barely hear her words. "It's okay," he said. "I'm here. I'm not pulling out."

"I'm so tired," she said.

"I know, I know," he said.

"Tired of being afraid."

"Shhh," David said.

"Help me," she said.

"I'm here. It's okay."

"Help me." She was crying. "Please. Make it stop."

"Shh," David said. "I'm here. I'm here."

Chapter 26

Constance's house looked the same from the outside. But the next day broke on a different feeling inside. A corner seemed to have been turned, or so it felt—maybe two corners.

Constance was awake as David entered. He opened the curtains and set a glass of water beside the several bottles of medication on the nightstand. He crawled on top of the covers and spooned her, nuzzled the back of her head.

"How do you feel about last night?" Constance said, facing away from him, smiling.

"Rescued," David said. "And you?"

"Like I have a reason to get out of bed." She turned to look at him. "Ironic, huh?"

It was time to decide. That much he knew. He had been given a blessed and no doubt brief reprieve from himself, his self-immolation, his long slide down. He had a clear head for a few hours—how long it would last, he didn't know. He had a chance to act, a chance to rectify. Maybe a last chance. He had to decide.

From his apartment, standing on the balcony, looking down on the murky pool, he made the first call.

Constance at about the same moment stood in her bathroom, in her bathrobe, at the shower. She turned the water on, then straightened up and didn't move for a long moment. Caught up in her thoughts, she bit her lip. Did what she was thinking make sense? It felt right, but did it make sense? She had some choices left; this was one of them. But it was an active choice, and did she not call herself an activist? It was a make-it-happen, not let-it-happen choice, something her father had always urged on her. She tried to catch her breath. She steadied herself on the corner of the shower. She reached in and turned the water off.

He had to talk it out. His caller, recognizing this was not a phone conversation, agreed to come to David's place.

They sat below David's apartment at the pool area, otherwise deserted at midday. David sat in a lounger, talking to his visitor on his right, a drink at his left. He was sober; the drink was iced tea.

"Let's say I get to Barcelona," he said. "I hide on a corner, waiting for a chance to speak with him. What will he see in me besides a rapist? What will his mother have told him to justify herself? Will he ever want to take a girl to meet his sexually deviant dad? No, I'll be his weak spot, the focus of soccer field jabs, embarrassed pride. There'll be late-night angst: 'What if I turn out like the old man?' "

Whatever he did next, Jamie was at the heart of it, he made clear to his interlocutor. There would always be other jobs—he could relocate and start anew;

he could find worth in doing volunteer work for other causes. But he had only one son. Which among his choices would redeem him in the boy's eyes? "I can't stand the idea of being his model for failure," he said.

Elderly Mrs. Hunter walked her dog, her beloved Irish setter with shining shampooed hair, past Constance's house. Talking companionably to the dog the whole way, ruffling his fur lovingly, she crossed the street at the end of the block and started back.

Indoors, Constance, still in her robe, put an armful of sheets into the washing machine off the kitchen alcove. She poured in laundry soap and fiddled with the controls. She stopped in the middle and leaned on the machine. She felt faint.

It was the house they had brought Jamie home to, a house of happiness for some years—not enough years. David was lying in the grass of the recently cut lawn of his former house, staring up through the leaves of the giant, sheltering ancient oak. The happiness had bled away—it was partly his own doing—the booze, the work mania, the unending social and political causes. Sharon found the life of an academic wife screamingly dull and confining.

The dashing, blade-smart philosophy professor she had met at a Washington symposium had captivated her at first, made her laugh, made her feel smart and loved. But she was a diplomat's daughter who had grown up all over the world, and she found Austin provincial. She was a woman with appetites, hungers that were answered rather poorly by the irritatingly solipsistic world of academic intellectuals debating

Heidegger and Husserl over wine spritzers. Vacations with her now-ambassador father in Madrid were a welcome escape. His was inarguably a more glamorous life. A Spanish architect she met on a visit to Barcelona began lavishing attentions on her, and he proved irresistible. She slipped into his bed. Home in Austin, she thought of little else and went back for more as soon as she could contrive to. Her relationship with David went from contentious to cold. Ending the marriage for Sharon was just a matter of time and opportunity. When David's troubles blossomed, the Spaniard provided the opportunity, with an offer of a more permanent arrangement, one that included her son of course. Sharon was greatly relieved to bail out and bid Texas *hasta la vista*. David was not wholly regretful to see her go, and it might have been a clean break for both sides, but for Jamie.

Constance's past life had been somewhat circumscribed by her nots: She was *not* going to be second because she was a woman; she was *not* going to trade on sex appeal; she was *not* going to subordinate her career to a man's, a husband's; she was *not* going to dress, think, or act in a manner shaped to please men; she was *not* going to be subservient to any man, in bed or out; she was *not* going to limit herself by thinking it was a man's world.

Ironically, most of those life resolves came from a man: her father.

Her timid stay-at-home mother had lived in the shadow of Constance's strong, well-meaning father, who wanted his daughter to have the same chance to be a world-beater as the son he never had. He was a corporate lawyer, tough, exacting, demanding of his daughter, and lavish in appreciation of her talents. He never said it, but no boyfriend she ever introduced to him measured up. She went on stoically, mostly alone, believing in the enabling power of excellence. Good things would come her way who was good enough. Good things did come her way—a formidable career, the regard of her peers, a wide range of loyal friends, professional honors. Many good things, but not a family. Nor a male life partner she could look up to in the unalloyed way of a daughter to a strong, adoring father.

Sorting through a box of memorabilia in her living room, Constance came across a picture of her father in his three-piece lawyer's suit, looking Establishment. Play between the lines, he liked to say. The old boy had hated the sixties for just that reason, she remembered. He had thought it one of the worst things ever to happen to this country. To him, it was not a period of rebellion against a government gone awry, nor a rebirth of some of the individualistic and humane values the country was founded on and designed to preserve. Hell, no. It was a destructive spree of indulgence by a generation of feckless dropouts. Like the lawyer he was, he believed in playing tough but playing inside the lines. Grow up, he'd said to his counterculture classmates; join the real world, be man enough to learn to work the system.

Constance found a photo of herself in her high school annual. She was mousy, intense. It was a portrait of a girl destined to toe the line, keep the ball in the court, accept the bad calls, and play on. With DeathWatch, she was her father's daughter: playing tenaciously but always by the rules, working to alter the system from within. Would what she was now contemplating meet with her father's approval? She thought not. It was divergent thinking; it was outside the norm. Would he understand that an unconventional act might accomplish what years and years of standard play had not? She was as scared by the thought of flouting her father's ghost as she was of the contemplated act itself. And as exhilarated.

The doorbell rang.

Mrs. Hunter stopped across the street while her dog peed on the ivy, and she watched the man at Constance's door. She saw Constance open the door to the man and saw the man nod and enter without taking off his cowboy hat. Mrs. Hunter was scandalized. What was the world coming to? That a man should enter a lady's house without taking off his hat! "Come along, Killer," she said to her silky Irish setter, and led him away.

David sat on the swing hanging from the ancient oak in front of his former house. He rocked slowly, staring at the dwelling, his mind a thousand days in the past. A yuppie woman opened the front door and stepped out, pulling her hair back a little nervously.

"Can I help you?" she said.

"No," David said, standing. "I'm sorry, just leaving. I'm sorry."

He walked to the curb, climbed in his car, and drove away without looking back. He continued his deep thinking. He ended up sitting in the Volvo in an unused corner parking lot at dusk. It rained. Night came on and he drank. He watched the water stream over the windshield and reviewed his options over and over. And drank. On the passenger seat sat Cloud Dog and a half-empty Black Bush bottle.

Hours later, in his sleeping stupor, he heard a voice call, "Time's up, bud." He was passed out, using Cloud Dog as a pillow, the bottle of Black Bush empty on the seat beside him. A light shined in on him, half waking him. A loud rap on the window with the flashlight finished the job. David sat up, blinded by the light. It was a cop. The cop gestured— it was time to move on.

Chapter 27

"Gale, time's up," the supervising guard said through the loudspeaker. Ellis Unit visitation hours were over.

That's it? It can't be. Bitsey was agitated. She was deep into David Gale's story and this was the end of it? All her storyteller's instincts told her that couldn't be the end. They had to keep on talking. She had to figure out what more happened. There were too many pieces still missing to leave it there.

David was drained.

"It was Dusty," Bitsey said. "He had a motive. He knew you both! He visited her that morning!"

He hushed her with his hand. "If I could answer for sure . . . we wouldn't be having this conversation," David said. "It's why I need you, why I chose you. Now I've told you everything."

"But I still don't know," Bitsey said.

The door guard approached from the rear, ready to take Gale back for the final time.

"I need more time," Bitsey said.

"You'll find time," David said.

"You should have done this earlier," Bitsey said, exasperation in her voice.

"You're not here to save me," David said with a matter-of-fact levelness that stunned Bitsey. The man was eerily calm. "You're here to save my son's memory of his father—that's all I want."

That, to Bitsey, was a shocking statement. In her mind, from the very beginning, she was there for no other reason than to save the man himself. She stared at him. She got a grip on her emotions. "You're going to let them kill you?" she said.

The condemned man stood up. "Bitsey, we spend our whole lives trying to stop death," he said. "Eating, inventing, loving, praying, fighting, killing—choose a verb. All to stop this evil, Job's 'king of terrors.' But what do we really know about death? Just that nobody comes back. There's a point . . . a moment . . . when your mind outlives its obsessions, when your habits survive your dreams, when your losses . . . You wonder, maybe death is a gift."

The door guard had waited long enough, even for a death row short-timer. "That's it," the door guard said. "Let's go, Gale."

David moved to the back of the cage to be hand-cuffed. "All I can tell you is that by this time tomorrow, I'll be dead," he said. "I know when. What I can't say is why." He stared at her.

Bitsey had become completely consumed by this man's plight. Confusion washed over her. Her feelings were pinballing out of control; her usual clearly defined role was in tatters. She had a panicky sense of losing her way.

The guard led the prisoner out of the cage.

"You have twenty-four hours to find out," David said, as the guard pulled him away. "Good-bye, Bitsey."

He was gone.

Bitsey stood. Frozen. Her heart pounding. She was unable to say good-bye. She stared after him until the iron door slammed shut. She stood there rigid, his remark churning in her head: *You're not here to save me. . . .*

In a late-afternoon thrumming rain, the rental car drove away from Ellis Unit for the last time. As the car reached the main highway, it passed a single protestor getting out of a van holding a sign: SAVE DAVID GALE. He raised the sign and it caught rain; its letters ran.

Zack, driving, sensed Bitsey's turmoil and shut up. He drove them out of town to a barbecue joint. Despite the rain, a crowd ate at picnic tables beneath a tin roof. The storm had let up somewhat, and the light drumming on the roof was soothing, or at least Zack thought so. They sat at one end of a long table and waited to be waited on. Zack said still not a word, watching a huge black chef spear slabs of ribs onto a large pit. Smoke blew through the patrons, but none of them seemed to mind.

Nor did Zack. Texas already felt less alien to him; it seemed perfectly natural to be sitting, breathing in hickory smoke and beef fat instead of air. This wasn't Upper West Side Manhattan. This was Deep East Texas and he had to stop himself from drawling his words when he talked. Here they don't analyze it— they just live it, he thought. A man could take a shine to this kind of—

"Zack!" Bitsey said, coming out of her funk, bringing him out of his reverie. "Go up and order."

Their dinners came and remained largely untouched while Bitsey gave Zack a rundown on the day's revelations. The barbecue smoke wafted past them. They fell silent again for a long, uncomfortable time.

"What time is it?" Bitsey said.

They paid and pointed the rental car back toward the motel. It was pouring rain again when they swung into the motel parking lot. As they emerged from the car and hurried toward their rooms, Braxton Belyeu got out of his car. Carrying Bitsey's umbrella and opening his own, he called out, "Miss Bloom!"

Bitsey held a newspaper over her head; Zack slouched in the downpour. They waited as the lawyer caught up with them.

"Any news from our video intruder friend?" Belyeu said.

Bitsey shook her head no.

Belyeu opened her umbrella and handed it to her. "Oh, I thought I'd return this," he said. "It's some weather."

"Any word on the appeal?" Bitsey said.

"Denied," Belyeu said. "Tape went to a federal judge two hours ago. What you got was definitely a snippet. Could be your video supplier friend has more nasty previews scheduled. Best not to get into too much sightseeing—just stick close to your motel room."

"How's David?" Bitsey said.

"Holdin' up," Belyeu said. "It'll be a hard night."

"Tell him I'll take care of it—about his son, I mean," Bitsey said. She was surprised to hear that promise pop out of her mouth. She hadn't planned to say it. She had a rule on stories: no promises, no personal involvements; do the story and move on.

"Will do," Belyeu said. "You stayin' for the execution?"

She nodded.

"Then I'll see you tomorrow," Belyeu said. "Watch yourselves."

They turned from one another.

Bitsey turned back. "Mr. Belyeu . . ." she said, calling after him.

He pivoted.

"Were Dusty and Constance close?" she said.

"Oh, yeah, thick as thieves, those two," Belyeu said.

"Lovers?" Bitsey said.

"Whoa, now you're plowing too close to the cotton, Bitsey." He considered it a beat. "That was just a rumor, nothin' else," he said. " 'Night." He turned again and strode quickly toward his car.

Bitsey and Zack exchanged a look.

Chapter 28

They were in Bitsey's room, sitting in the dark on either side of a table, looking out the window. Rain shadows streaked their faces. The motel phone was on the table between them, as was Zack's watch: 10:17 P.M.

It was a vigil of sorts. Not intentionally so, but they were both thinking through the probable last night on earth of a person who now had a face and a smile and a tone of voice.

Yes, just another story, Bitsey thought to herself, but she had never been called upon to get next to a soon-to-be-dead interview subject. She had never had to confront the nakedness of the imminent, intentional killing of a person she had come to know and, despite herself, care about. Would she have taken the assignment had she seen this coming? Never, she thought, never. It was tapping into some sort of primordial fellow feeling that had probably saved the human race from killing itself off long since. She had been called upon to play a role—there was no other way to say it, it was what she felt—to play a part in the extinguishing of a human life. It was too grave, too heavy to bear. She was sickened.

*   *   *

Zack fell asleep in his clothes at the foot of one of the beds. The rain lightened up outside. The lights in the motel restaurant went off one by one. The lights in the other motel rooms went on, then one by one started to go off. The light in Bitsey's room dimmed but stayed on.

Bitsey, her shoes off, sat on the floor, leaning against the other bed. On her own bed was her neatly packed suitcase. She was watching the death video and taking notes.

On her notepad, she had sketched a flowchart of the videotape with major elements timed out. She watched it from beginning to end, then rewound and started over. Again and again. She had watched it so many times now, she no longer saw anything. She watched it again.

Travelers on the rainswept interstate, were they to glance over, could have seen that all the windows in the Huntsville Motel were dark except the one. From that one, the flickering blue glow of the television continued on and on.

The early light of a fog-shrouded morning crept up behind the giant redbrick walls of the Huntsville Unit. In the inner courtyard, where night seemed to linger and dawn came later, a TDCJ van slowly pulled through large iron gates, its headlights blinding the guards inside for a second or two.

The van came from Ellis Unit, fifteen miles away, and carried a condemned inmate destined for the Death House.

It was Friday, Gale's scheduled execution day. Six thirty p.m. was the appointed time, fewer than twelve hours away. Until then, practically every mo-

ment for him scripted, every movement choreo-
graphed. There were official final day procedures,
and prison officials would stick to them rigidly. The
officials and guards wouldn't deny it, the killing of
a prisoner was an emotional and trying event for
them too, and sticking to a routine and avoiding surprises made it easier to get through.

Even so, the process took its toll. Guards sought
counsel with the prison chaplain more frequently in
the days leading up to executions. The mood among
employees in the administrative offices turned tense
and withdrawn. The warden's longtime secretary, at
the end of a recent month during which there were
six executions, started crying hysterically on an evening approaching a seventh, then began to vomit uncontrollably. Her duties on execution day were to
stay in the office taking progress reports by telephone
on the state and behavior of the prisoner, and to
monitor the status of any last-minute appeals. She
had reached her breaking point. A Muslim chaplain,
asked by a prisoner to be present in the Death House
on his last day as his religious listener and prayer
leader, walked outside on a break and, beaded with
sweat, whispered to the regular Death House chaplain, "This is the most frightening thing I've ever
been involved in."

The TDCJ van rolled slowly to the far side of the
courtyard. Armed prison guards waited. They were
on full alert, hands on their weapons, fingers on the
safeties. This was a sensitive moment, the transfer
from the Ellis Unit van into Huntsville Unit. It was
the condemned's last contact with the earth's fresh
air, his last touch of nature, his last look at the sky
if he chose to take it. After the transfer, he would

never again lay eyes on anything but gray-blue prison walls and concrete floors. He would walk his last few steps and draw his last breath in sterile institutional halls and chambers. An attempt to break free, even if only to trigger sudden and merciful suicide by cop, could happen at this juncture.

The Huntsville guards' adrenaline was flowing as the van from Ellis Unit came to a stop. A transport officer came around and unlocked the back door. He swung it open. Three Ellis Unit officers got out, followed by David—he was shackled at his ankles and wrists. He looked calm. He took a deep breath of the air, and he didn't resist. He looked around briefly—at the courtyard, the guards, the walls—as they led him to a green door at the side of a redbrick building. He checked out the face of the building as he approached and entered, curious, not uninterested. This was building 1835. This was the Huntsville Death House.

Fog muted the ever-present whoosh of vehicles passing on the interstate. It was still early morning; no activity showed at the Huntsville Motel. The only part of the sign that was lit was the NO VACANCY sign.

A door to a second-tier room opened, and a couple stepped out on the gangway. Young, blue-collar, half asleep, wearing matching KILL GALE T-shirts, they clumped past Bitsey's quiet room. They were on their way for a nice healthy breakfast before driving in and joining the capital punishment front lines. Somebody had to carry the flag.

At their heavy-tread passing, Bitsey woke with a start in her room. She was still sitting on the floor, slumped against the bed. She looked around, getting her bearings. There was static on the TV. She leaned over and turned it off. Standing, rubbing her eyes, she peered at the alarm clock on the nightstand. She stepped around the feet extending off the end of the bed, the sleeping Zack.

She looked at herself in the mirror in the bathroom. Exhausted, heavyhearted, she wearily brushed her teeth. Glancing down, she saw the towel left on the floor. She picked it up and was starting to hang it on the towel rack when she stopped and looked up at herself in the mirror. Something nagged at her, clawing up from her subconscious. She held still a moment. Then a picture snapped into focus—just a picture, a slightly odd discrepancy, then more, then an idea with the force of a freight train. She spat out the toothpaste and ran into the bedroom.

"Zack!" Bitsey said, putting on her shoes. "Wake up! Get up!"

He started to pull himself awake.

"Did you throw the towel on the floor?" Bitsey said. She was keyed up.

"What?" Zack said, groggy, disoriented. He stumbled to his feet.

"The towel on my bathroom floor," Bitsey said. "Did you throw it there?"

"Yeah, I guess," Zack said. "It's a motel room. What . . . ?"

"Do you do that at home?" Bitsey said. She was hurriedly unplugging the VCR.

"No," Zack said. "Fuck, Bitsey. I'm sorry. It's not like it's . . ."

"Get up," Bitsey said. She got the VCR disconnected and picked it up.

"What the fuck's wrong with you?" Zack said.

"Grab the TV," she said. " I want to check something."

"What?" Zack said.

"We're taking a tour," she said.

"Where?" Zack said.

She had the VCR under one arm. She grabbed her purse on the way to the door. "Austin," Bitsey said. "Get the TV." She yanked the door open and charged out.

Chapter 29

It was a fast trip, Bitsey driving like a New York cabdriver, passing cars and trucks on the two lanes, swearing at lumbering road tortoises to get the hell out of her way.

Zack hung on, half amused at her mania and half terrified that she'd get them both killed. What possessed her? He had not seen this side of Bitsey Bloom—obsessed, fixated, pulling out all the stops. She was pushing it right to the edge, not the control freak he thought her to be to the core.

Nor would she shed light on the darkness. She refused to go into any detail about what was coming, what was so important in Austin.

They crossed the Austin city limits, careened down the interregional highway, and veered off at the last U.T. exit. They flashed past the University and through one of the residential faculty-housing areas. At the familiar run-down section on the far periphery, Bitsey pulled the rental car up in front of 3307, Goth Girl's house—formerly the home of Constance Harraway, now deceased.

With Bitsey carrying the VCR, Zack hefting the

motel TV, they mounted the front porch. Bauhaus music pounded through the door. They rang the bell. The music went down, and after a long pause, Goth Girl answered the door, wearing only a NINE INCH NAILS T-shirt that barely covered her oversized butt.

Bitsey barged in past her, carrying the VCR, with Zack in hot pursuit lugging the TV. "Wanna make a hundred bucks?" Bitsey said.

"What do I gotta do?" the Goth Girl said languidly. There was no hesitation in her answer, as though it was not unusual for people to show up with kinky requests and not unusual for her to comply.

"We're going over the crime scene," Bitsey said, entering the living room, with Zack and Goth Girl close behind. She trooped on into the kitchen. She walked around, checking it out. She noticed one thing different. The tripod was back. The other exhibit pieces hadn't changed.

"And for the next hour I want you do *exactly* what I say *when* I say to do it," Bitsey said. "If I say, 'Suck Zack's dick,' all I want to hear from you is, 'Would you like me to swallow?' "

"You want me to suck his dick?" Goth Girl said, a faint note of hesitation entering her voice for the first time.

"It's just a figure of speech," Zack said, stunned yet again by a Bitsey who was new to him. He almost swallowed his tongue. Clearly he didn't know the half of this woman. Maybe there was a reason she was at the top of the heap in her profession.

"Is your boyfriend here?" Bitsey said.

"He ain't exactly my boyfriend anymore," Goth Girl said with a kind of detached wistfulness.

"Well, is his video camera here?" Bitsey said.

"Yeah," Goth Girl said.

"Get it," Bitsey said.

Goth Girl started to leave, then turned back. "I gotta collect first," she said, lingering in the kitchen door. She stood limply, hands hanging at her side, waiting to be activated by money.

"Zack, give her the money," Bitsey said.

One forty-eight the stereo clock read. Zack's hand entered the frame, as seen through Goth Girl's ex-boyfriend's video camera, and turned the music down.

Zack was the videographer, moving and adjusting the image of the kitchen crime scene at 3307. He zoomed the lens in to a perspective similar to that on the Constance tape. The exhibit pieces—kitchen gloves, handcuffs, duct tape roll—were more or less in proper position. Goth Girl removed pizza boxes and laundry from the counter.

"Take out the index cards," Zack said from behind the lens.

Goth Girl picked up the index cards and put them out of camera range.

Zack looked up from the video camera's eyepiece. The camera, fixed on the tripod where it had been at the time of the murder, was connected to Goth Girl's TV and transmitting a live image to it.

Beside it, Bitsey had set up the motel TV and VCR with the Constance tape. She cued the Constance tape to the beginning and froze the image.

Zack compared that image to the video camera angle on Goth Girl's TV.

"Zoom in, but not much," Bitsey said.

He did so.

Bitsey compared perspectives between the live image—Goth Girl cleaning—on the left-hand TV to the image on the Constance tape on the right-hand TV.

"Put the gloves on a dish rack," Bitsey said.

"I don't have one," the Goth Girl said.

Zack went to the sink, laid three pizza boxes on the counter as an ersatz dish rack, and draped the kitchen gloves over them.

"Turn them inside out," Bitsey said. "Move the duct tape about a foot to the left. And get rid of the handcuffs."

He performed all three actions.

Bitsey turned to Goth Girl. "Could you . . . What's your name?" she said.

"Nico's cool," Goth Girl said.

"Nico, lie down facing the counter," Bitsey said.

Nico sat on the floor and started to take off her T-shirt.

"We can imagine that part, thank you," Bitsey said. "Put her in position," she said to Zack.

Zack, checking the freeze frame on the tape, arranged Nico in the position of Constance—which now bore no relation to the white outline on the floor.

"That's fine," Bitsey said. "Just straighten her legs."

Zack and Bitsey looked at the two TV images. They were almost identical.

"Okay, look at this," Bitsey said, putting the Constance tape in PLAY mode. Nothing moved on the tape, but the red digital numbers began rolling over on the VCR. "I noticed this back at the motel. See?"

Bitsey touched the TV screen by one of Constance's feet. The foot moved ever so slightly. Bitsey hit pause. "She moves her foot," Bitsey said. "Why? It's another fifteen seconds before she comes to. If she had passed out once, that would have been it. She wouldn't come back."

Zack thought about it. "Maybe she was faking, hoping he'd go away," he said.

"Or . . ." Bitsey said. She didn't finish her thought, but clearly she had another explanation in mind, some other way to explain that movement in someone who appeared to have lost consciousness and was close to death from asphyxiation. She looked over at Nico. "We've got to bag her," she said.

"Whoa," Zack said. "We're going a little too far here, Bitsey."

"Okay," Bitsey said. "Then I'll do it."

Chapter 30

From his DeathWatch days, David Gale knew the drill in the Huntsville Death House in detail, well before there was any remote possibility he might experience it himself.

He knew before they led him in that the Death House holding cell was a barred cage with open visibility on three sides. That the condemned person, by strict prison rules, had to be watched in his final hours by at least two correctional officers at all times. He knew that the officers would keep their distance at the end of the room, but that the chaplain, ready to interact as much as the prisoner desired, would stay close by the cell.

In earlier days, David had had enough conversations with the Death House chaplain to know that at Huntsville, his role was key. He was the meeter and greeter, the all-day companion and the carbon rod sunk into the atomic pile to absorb excess nuclear particles and prevent detonation. There to receive the prisoner when he was vanned in from death row, the chaplain's job was to establish a rapport that ideally would hold through the man's last breath.

The Reverend Stephen M. Lipman, the regular Huntsville prison chaplain, had been dragged unwillingly by the warden into serving as the Death House chaplain when executions resumed in 1982. His stated function was to comfort the prisoner on his dying day; his unstated role was to do whatever he could think of to keep the prisoner from fighting back. Rev. Lipman agreed to the unsavory duty solely on the basis of his compassionate belief that no man, however evil, should have to die alone.

The reverend had been offered three bits of advice by a Death House chaplain from the earlier era: follow his heart, never promise anything he couldn't deliver, and always deliver what he promised. With that as a starting point, he contrived a system that worked most of the time.

As soon as the prisoner got settled in the holding cell, the reverend would recite the day's agenda, right up to the moment at six p.m. when the prisoner would be led away to die. There would be no surprises. Even the death knell was scripted: "It's time to go," the reverend would say—no more, no less.

Gale, as a death-penalty critic, was aware that Rev. Lipman and the prison officials at Huntsville strove to make an inherently barbarous act humane. The one small, high-up window in the Death House holding-cell area was a source of anguish to prisoners; when the sliver of light and sky began to change and darken as the day waned, signaling the end, it sent inmates into a tailspin. Lipman had the window painted over black, and made sure the light was constant and even all day long.

The officials strove to keep the Death House quiet. A major aggravation to prison inmates was the incessant cacophony of the cell blocks—the all-day noise assault from boom boxes, rap music, talking, screaming, bar banging, the roar of TV sports. Once in the Death House, they were soothed by the silence.

As the official arranger and traffic cop, Rev. Lipman escorted family, friends, and spiritual advisers in and out for final visits with the condemned. Inmate David Gale had only one visitor all day—his lawyer.

The reverend placed phone calls for the prisoners, handing the phone in through the bars. David made no phone calls nor received any.

The reverend was there to help the prisoner write letters and compose and rehearse his final words. David of all people needed no help in those departments. But neither did he write any letters or compose any final words.

David knew the rest of the drill so well, the chaplain did not have to recite it.

After visiting time was over, he would be led in for a shower, relieved of his white prison jumpsuit, and given the civilian clothes he would wear for his death. Why a shower before death? David had never really wanted to know the answer to that.

For his last meal, David knew not to order Supremes de Volaille and Chateauneuf du Pap; he knew it had to be something from the usual prison menu, something the kitchen would have. His long-since-chosen last meal would be well within the reach of the prison chefs.

Dutifully, Rev. Lipman offered to pray with David, or read him religious passages from whatever holy book he desired. Christian inmates often requested the Thirty-ninth Psalm: "Lord, make me to know mine end, and the measure of my days. . . . And now Lord, what wait I for? My hope is in thee." And the last: "O spare me, that I may recover strength, before I go hence, and be no more."

David respectfully declined; whatever religion he practiced was between himself and his god.

In fact, Rev. Lipman, for all his experience with Death House inmates, could not read David Gale at all. He did not seem spiritually bereft or despairing or depressed. Willing as Lipman was, there seemed nothing he could offer Gale.

Still, he remained attentive and on the alert, for the hardest part was fast approaching. The possibility always loomed of the prisoner—even the most composed prisoner—going ballistic at the end.

When the clock hit six, Lipman would say, "It's time to go," and he and the tie-down team—two or three guards—would escort Gale from the holding cell across a five-yard space to the metal door of the death chamber, a twelve-by-sixteen room. Once inside, Gale would be helped onto the gurney and tied down hand and foot with white restraining straps, his arms extended on flat, narrow boards, his hands taped down with adhesive tape.

It was at this point that the toughest, proudest, most steadfastly resigned individuals could lose it. Fear erupted in their eyes; tears welled. Some began screaming and struggling to rise from the gurney and break free.

The impresarios of an execution would do anything to avoid such a scene. Not only was it upsetting to all involved—including the witnesses who were waiting behind the curtain to observe the final moment—but having to hold a screaming, panicking man down while you pumped him full of killer chemicals made the whole procedure seem, well, barbaric: Death House staffers prayed that it would go smoothly, prayed that the condemned man would let himself be knocked off in a "civilized" manner.

Chaplain Lipman quietly went over the details of the actual execution with David, to avoid any possible surprises. David sat on the edge of his bunk listening politely as the chaplain talked.

Medical techs would place IVs in his arm. Two phones in the chamber would have open lines in case of a last-minute reprieve—one to the governor's office, and one to the attorney general. Technicians behind three small windows in the chamber would ready the lethal chemicals. Lipman himself would pull back the curtain to let the witnesses behind the brass rail see him and he them. David could then say his last words and last good-byes. The signal for the injections to begin would be the warden's removing his glasses. Breathe out at that point, the reverend advised David, clear the lungs, and he would go to sleep more quickly—usually within seven to twelve seconds.

Two guards watched the prisoner as the chaplain finished his recitation, alert to any change in demeanor, any hint of trouble to come.

Belyeu was on the wall phone on the other side of the bars, talking to his office in Austin. "Thank you, Bobbi," Belyeu said. "Thank you." He hung up and turned to David. "Supreme Court death clerk gave the go-ahead," he said.

David looked from Belyeu to the guards. He nodded slowly. His expression betrayed neither surprise nor dismay. He seemed quite composed.

*   *   *

At the 3307 house in Austin, Bitsey and Zack stood by the sink, waiting, Bitsey looking at her watch. They looked up expectantly as Nico hurried into the kitchen.

"I found it." She held up the small key to the handcuffs and handed it to Zack.

Zack tried the key in the cuffs to make sure it worked, then laid cuffs and key on the sink counter. Also on the counter were a white plastic bag and, beside it, the roll of duct tape.

"Okay, I want you to wait three minutes before you take the bag off," Bitsey said to Zack.

"Bitsey, I'm really not so sure about this," Zack said.

"Three *full* minutes," Bitsey said. "Just stand behind the tripod. Both of you."

Zack and Nico moved behind the tripod, where the video camera was still rolling, recording it all.

Bitsey put the bag on her head and ripped off a long length of tape. She sealed the bag around her neck.

At that point, Zack began timing on his watch.

Bitsey handcuffed herself, hands behind her, with some difficulty. The key was visible on the sink counter the whole while she did this. "Have you started?" she said to Zack, through the bag.

"Twenty-two seconds," Zack said.

Bitsey sat down on the linoleum, then lay on her side.

Zack started to count the seconds aloud. Thirty . . . Forty . . .

Bitsey lay perfectly still.

Fifty seconds . . . One minute . . .

Bitsey pulled at the cuffs slightly.

"Maybe she shouldn't . . ." Nico said.

The count continued. One ten . . . One twenty . . . One thirty . . .

Bitsey was starting to panic. She fought the cuffs. One fifty . . .

Nico the Goth Girl, Embracer of Darkness and Spawn of Satan, was starting to panic also. "This isn't cool," she whimpered.

"Zack!" Bitsey said, through the bag.

Zack ran to her, knocking over the tripod. He ripped the bag open. She sucked air. He ripped the tape off her mouth.

"Jesus fucking Christ!" Zack said. "You okay?"

She tried to catch her breath.

Nico crouched down and unlocked the handcuffs.

"No more fucking experiments, all right?" Zack said. "Just tell me what's going on. You okay?"

Bitsey nodded and held up her hand, wanting to say something. She took his arm, looked at him. Breathing heavily, she rasped, "She . . . she did it herself."

Less than three hours left in the life of David Gale.

One eighth of one day left of breathing and thinking for a man who lived for thinking and would die for an act he could barely imagine. He sat in the Death House holding cell, somber but composed, sorting through a meager collection of personal effects.

He took a postcard with a picture of San Francisco from his box of things.

A guard checked the lining of the prisoner's Yale sweatshirt and handed it to Belyeu.

David studied the back of the postcard. It read:

I'm sorrier than you can know—Berlin, the student who would do anything.

He held it in his hands for a long moment, staring at nothing. With a look of resolve, he handed the postcard to the guard to be checked.

The fate of David Gale, the explanation of how he got to the brink of an ignominious death by injection, was the sole topic of intense speculation and discussion at Constance's former house.

Zack sat on the couch in the living room, holding the handcuffs and smoking nervously.

Goth Girl Nico, now humanly invested in a story that before was just a kick and a meal ticket, sat on one of the armrests.

Bitsey paced in front of them. "She used the gloves to keep fingerprints off the tape and bag," she said. "Then she put them back on the dish rack, but upside down and inside out, a housewives' habit. A murderer would have just tossed them aside—like they were the first time we were here"—she looked at Zack—"like you do with a towel in a crap motel."

"Maybe," Zack said thoughtfully. "All right, *maybe*." He indicated the cuffs. "But why wear these?"

"They threw me," Bitsey said. "I forgot you have to have the key to put them on. But she needed them. She knew she would instinctively try to rip the bag off, that at some point automatism would kick in."

"Fuckin' A, like when people hang themselves," Goth Girl said. "At the last second they go chicken, claw at the rope and their neck and shit. The cops find their own skin beneath their nails."

"And she swallowed the key so she couldn't get to it," Bitsey said. "She made sure there was no way out."

"Whoa," Zack said. "Why *not* hang yourself or take pills? Why take your fucking clothes off? Why make it look like a murder?"

A long silence. Bitsey knew that was the key question, and without a good answer, her whole house-of-cards theory tumbled. "It's so calculated," she said. "She's handcuffed, taped at the mouth. The gloves. The damn tripod."

"Why, Bitsey?" Zack said. "Why fake your own murder? It doesn't make sense. The woman's a bleeding-heart abolitionist. Why frame an innocent man? Why send Gale to the chair for what looks—"

"What?" Bitsey said.

"She had to know *some* innocent fuck would take the fall," Zack said.

"Oh, my God, Zack, that's it!" Bitsey said. "That's why!" She practically jumped off the ground. "To prove it happens! To have *absolute* proof that the system convicts innocents."

"Get the fuck out of here," Zack said.

"No, that's how she thought," Bitsey said. "She lived for DeathWatch. If she's gonna die anyway, why not die for *it*? That's why the tripod was here. To record proof, undeniable proof, the tape. That's why we got an outtake."

"A dead woman put the tape in your room?" Zack said.

"Of course not," Bitsey said. "She needed help, someone to keep it, release it. Someone she could trust, someone dedicated to the cause . . ."

They stared at each other for a beat. The same thought.

"As thick as thieves," Bitsey and Zack said at the same moment.

Chapter 31

Dusty Wright—the Cowboy—lived by himself in a cabin near the edge of some woods, a good way out of Huntsville in the Sam Houston National Forest. The cabin was back off a country road and secluded. Climbing up through the woods to approach from the rear, Bitsey and Zack took a vantage point several dozen yards back in the shadows of the trees. The cabin looked comfortable, in a rough and rustic way. The big gray pickup was parked beside it in the gravel entrance drive. The cabin's windows were open to the muggy afternoon. There wasn't another human dwelling within eye- or earshot. It was a peaceful, idyllic, remote spot.

Dusty was inside—they could see him sitting in a rocker, listening to the strains of a Verdi opera, his eyes closed. Through the open windows they could hear the lovely, emotional "Quando le sere al placido" from *Luisa Miller*.

"Fuckin' freak," Zack said.

They saw him check his pocket watch. Bitsey did the same: 4:23 P.M.

"Come on," she whispered, turning back into the woods, leading Zack away.

They emerged from the woods at the back of the parking lot of a long-abandoned bowling alley. It was about a quarter mile through the trees from the Cowboy's cabin to this junky stretch of lonely highway. They had parked the rental car beneath a fifties-era sign of a large bowling pin with peeling white paint. They stood by the car scraping off the mud that covered their shoes.

"Because of the Berlin thing," Bitsey said, "Constance knew the police would go straight to Gale. In a way, he's the perfect innocent. Smart. Articulate. Telegenic."

"And a high-profile alcoholic whose life was shit," Zack said. "There's only one problem."

"I know," Bitsey said. "She was half in love with him."

They got in the car.

"Dusty's a bullhorner," Bitsey said, "a zealot who's OD'd on too many good causes." She was thinking out loud, looking for the right way to fit all the pieces of the puzzle together.

"They fired him from DeathWatch and the ACLU," Zack said. "The guy was starting to act crazier than the enemy."

"Right," Bitsey said. That fit. The picture was coming into focus. "The plan was probably for Dusty to release the tape after Gale's conviction, after a year or so. It would force Gale to dry out, give him back his dignity. So Dusty Wright is sitting on this tape, waiting. He's the only one who knows about it. So good ol' Dusty starts to think that an erroneous execution is a lot more politically useful than a last-minute save."

"Because a last-minute save," Zack said with rising interest, "would only prove that the system works."

"Almost-martyrs don't count," Bitsey said. She put herself in Dusty's shoes, looking at Gale's execution as he must be seeing it. "After all, what's one murder if it stops thousands?"

"And he's jealous of Gale anyway," Zack said. "That wasn't Dusty's semen they found in Constance."

"Constance has sex with Gale," Bitsey said with irony, "so Dusty fucks them both."

"So he'll release the whole tape only after the execution?" Zack said.

Bitsey nodded, thinking about that. "Which means," she said, "he must have the original somewhere. What time is it?"

This was not an easy time for Dusty. He believed in what he was doing, but he had a heart, too. He had emotions that welled up easily and got out of control. He had to guard against that. It was the purpose the music served for him—to keep him level, to soothe, to tamp down his anger, to help him ride out the extreme swings of rage or weeping sentimentality that sometimes gripped him

Volatile as a kid, he had been tipped over the edge by a short, disastrous stint in Vietnam at a young age. He was at Plei Me in the Central Highlands, early in the war, with a platoon of dirt-kickers like himself. And happy to be there. Until then a loner, he had fallen in with a like-minded crew of hayseeds the minute he got sent in-country. Suddenly he belonged. Until Ia Drang. Six of his eight buddies got blown away by heavy automatic weapons fire the first day of the battle of LZ X-Ray. The seventh guy got sent home without half his neck and mouth.

Dusty was untouched, physically, but he crawled in a mud bunker within a couple of days and wouldn't come out of it. He was sent home with severe post-traumatic stress disorder after an army shrink watched him cry uncontrollably when an F-4 Phantom did a high-speed pass over the base that rattled the infirmary windows.

Now, sitting in his quiet country cabin, listening to one of his most beloved Puccini arias, "Un Bel Di" from *Madame Butterfly*, he was fighting agitation. He was trying to find in the music some magic counter-balance to the violence about to be perpetrated in Huntsville, violence in which he had a role.

He flipped open his fob watch and checked it against the wall clock: 4:50. He heard the phone ring over the aria. He turned down the music and picked up the phone. "Hello?" he said.

At a defunct and isolated gas station not too far down the country road from Dusty's cabin, a single streetlight burned through the late-afternoon fog, putting a halo of light around the phone booth directly beneath it. Zack spoke into the phone with the door open. Bitsey stood just outside by the rental car.

"Let's talk about your tape," Zack said, his voice a little gruff to hide his nervousness. He paused to let that sink in. As soon as Dusty started to respond, Zack went on. "No, meet me at the gas station down the hill in fifteen minutes." He hung up before Dusty could object or argue. He stepped out of the booth and shot Bitsey a tentative look.

Bitsey slid into the driver's seat of the rental car. Zack stayed by the phone booth. "Don't move from the booth," she said. "Call the second you see his pickup. Remember, let it ring just once. Then get into the woods."

"I know," Zack said. "Go."

"Into the woods, Zack," Bitsey said, starting the car.

"Go!" Zack said.

She put it into gear and sped away, throwing some dust and gravel from the gas station driveway.

In his cabin, Dusty hung the phone up and didn't move right away. He knew who was calling. He sorted through the possibilities of what they might do. He looked at his watch. He made a tactical decision and moved quickly to act on it.

Chapter 32

The gable clock read 5:04.

In the media area outside the Huntsville Unit, now crowded with press reporters and TV units, a CNN reporter was doing a stand-up, with the Death House and its gable clock as backdrop.

"Constance Harraway and David Gale," the professionally earnest, perfectly coifed young woman said, "but for their tragic and personal involvement in this story would have been pleased to see that an execution has at last engendered such a high level of worldwide interest. Although pressure appears to be mounting in certain quarters in the U.S. to put a moratorium on executions while the practice can be reviewed, it remains to be seen whether any of this"—she gestured around at the media horde—"even appears on the radar screens in Washington. . . ."

If the presence of writers from the *New York Times*, *Washington Post*, *Boston Globe*, *Chicago Tribune*, and *Los Angeles Times*, along with network correspondents from the Big Three networks and the cable news outlets, along with reporters from *Le Monde*, the *London Times*, and a half dozen other major inter-

national papers—if their presence were any indica-
tion, then David Gale's execution would indeed
make a blip on the radar screens in D.C. A very
bright light would be shining on U.S. death penalty
policy for the next few news cycles.

Several DeathWatch volunteers were present with
protest signs, but they were not vocal. Their hearts
were painfully conflicted. Constance Harraway had
been their much-loved friend and leader. David Gale
was about to be executed for murdering her. Their
hatred for him ran deep. And yet principle had to
prevail. If they truly believed the death penalty
should be abolished, they couldn't very well welcome it just this once because they had a personal
stake.

A coalition of international campaigners against
the death penalty were trying to make a big media
noise, with the deputy director of the United Nations
Human Rights Commission taping an interview for
Good Morning America. The director of the Program
to Abolish the Death Penalty for Amnesty International was handing out copies of the Universal Declaration of Human Rights, pointing out that the death
penalty violated the declaration's tenets of a right
to life and a prohibition against cruel, inhuman, or
degrading punishment. A pair of legal scholars on
capital punishment offered opinions about the Supreme Court's leanings. "This is the most favorable
term in a quarter of a century in terms of death penalty jurisprudence," the executive director of the National Coalition to Abolish the Death Penalty said to
a *Time* magazine correspondent. A Columbia University law professor opined to an MSNBC camera that
recent court rulings "suggest the court has heard the

public raising questions about the death penalty, and it is prepared, like the rest of us, to rethink the issue."

Constance Harraway would never hear these encouraging words; whether David Gale ever would seemed very, very unlikely.

The Texas Department of Criminal Justice, Huntsville Unit, was functioning efficiently and smoothly on game day. All the players had showed up rested and ready; all the individuals were serving the interests of the team. The climactic minutes of the day were approaching.

In the Huntsville Unit kitchen, the script was being followed: the handwritten menu for David Gale's last meal:

Four pancakes. Maple syrup. Fresh strawberries. Whipped cream. Chocolate shavings (extra chocolate). Earl Grey tea. Milk.

Outside, Duke Grover stepped out of the Huntsville Unit Welcome House and walked to the platform at the head of the press area. He had done this drill over two hundred times before—standing in front of a battery of microphones briefing the media on the execution du jour. "All executions in Texas," he began, "take place at six p.m. . . . "

Within the Walls on the afternoon a prisoner was scheduled to die, a hush descended over the cell blocks. Radios, TVs, boom boxes were shut down; inmates spoke in muted voices instead of shouting.

Whether they knew the unlucky dude or not, the rest of the populace offered up their silence as respect.

In the kitchen, the cook staff attended quietly to their special charge. A man's Last Meal had an aura about it. Far from taking it lightly, the staff took it as a kind of sacred trust, to be performed as precisely and as well as possible. The idea of a Final Meal was so concrete and so vivid that each man could imagine himself in the skin of the person about to die—could imagine sitting at a table staring at his plate thinking, This is the last time I will ever eat, the last food I will ever taste. The kitchen staff labored to send off a well-made meal as a kind of gift to the departing.

The job of the dutiful Section 1835 guard, a dour West Texan named Lowell, was to read the menu list aloud, ticking off the items on prisoner David Gale's list. A Hispanic inmate cook wearing a hairnet and plastic gloves poured syrup over the pancakes. "Maple syrup," the inmate cook said.

"Maple syrup," the Section 1835 guard said.

"Fresh strawberries: large," the inmate cook said.

"Fresh strawberries: large," the Section 1835 guard said.

Out in the open-air press area, Grover continued his official description of the process. He had made this speech many times before, but never for so large and attentive an audience. He spoke in a rote manner, making the proceedings sound as routine and impersonal as changing a flat tire or adjusting a carburetor.

"Once the witnesses are brought into the execution facility," he said, "a curtain is pulled, and after completion of last words, the injection is administered."

In the kitchen, the Section 1835 guard and the inmate cook continued their jobs.

"Reddi-wip whipped cream," the inmate cook said.

"Reddi-wip whipped cream," the Section 1835 guard said.

Media types scribbled notes as Grover talked. Local video remotes fed pictures of his spiel live and the networks taped.

"Sodium thiopentothal for sedation purposes," Grover droned, "puts you to sleep, basically. Pancuronium bromide to collapse the diaphragm and lungs. Potassium chloride to stop the heart."

Several shouts of "Spell it, please!" for the sodium thiopentothal and pancuronium bromide. Grover obliged.

The kitchen staff were proceeding to the end of their checklist and getting ready to hand off.

"Chocolate shavings, extra serving," the inmate cook said.

"Chocolate shavings, extra serving," the Section 1835 guard said.

"Earl Grey tea," the inmate cook said.

"Earl Grey tea," the Section 1835 guard said.

"Milk," the inmate cook said.

"Milk," the Section 1835 guard said.

The final meal was assembled on a tray. The inmate cook did a couple of last tweakings of the food's presentation—straightening up the stack of pancakes, adding another strawberry and another dollop of whipped cream. He stepped back and stripped off his plastic gloves.

The Section 1835 guard nodded to an inmate server, who stepped forward and picked up the tray.

*   *   *

"The whole cocktail," Grover said, bringing the formal part of his presentation to a close, "costs the state of Texas eighty-six dollars and eight cents per elimination."

Hands started waving and the eager-beaver media corps started shouting questions: Would Gale be wearing a diaper? Had he shaved in the last few days? Do most men shave before going to their death? Why? With whom was Gale spending his last hours? Had his ex-wife and son come to visit and/or were they present now? Would his son be allowed to witness the execution if he *were* present?

Grover, the media corps' least favorite kind of spokesgeek, had long since learned to answer as many questions as he could with a simple yes or no.

Chapter 33

Bitsey got back to the bowling alley parking lot with about two minutes of breakneck driving. She parked the car in the shadows and lit out through the woods. She arrived at a vantage point from which she could see Dusty Wright's cabin just in time.

She saw Dusty bang out the front door and go striding down off the porch. Without looking left or right, he jumped into the pickup, keyed the ignition, and spun out of the driveway.

Bitsey hurried to the front door. She tried it—unlocked. She walked in.

The cabin was rough and bare. She moved slowly across the plank floor, past piles of old newspapers, a small, threadbare Turkish rug, dingy swaybacked furniture. It was a spare and simple living space, testament to an ascetic, antimaterialistic frame of mind. The one conspicuous concession to comfort and pleasure was a latest-generation sound system, with a tower of Puccini and other classical CDs

Bitsey turned, scanning the walls. They were a testament of another kind. This was not a man to whom the word "conventional" would be applied across the board, she thought. This was a man obsessed. He had an idée fixe, which was death by execution, which looked in some sense to have taken over his life.

On one wall was an old 1930s poster for the I.W.W.—the International Workers of the World—the Wobblies. Okay, nothing off the charts there. But the rest of the wall ornamentation was stunning: a lithograph of the 1928 *Daily News* photo of Ruth Snyder's execution, her helmeted head stiffened in death; Tiny Davis, blood pouring from his mouth from 2,300 volts, seated in Old Sparky in Florida, an eight-inch-thick leather strap restraining his huge shaved head; photographs of lynchings in Georgia and Tennessee.

Perforce, these were daily reminders—all-day reminders—to Dusty of man's inhumanity to man. But what a macabre gallery of indignation it was, Bitsey thought. What kind of person would want to live with such stuff, which created its own terrifying obscenity?

And Dusty's friends—if he had any—what must they be like who could come and sit in view of such raw pain?

Tearing her eyes from the walls, Bitsey inspected the bookshelves. A section of videos caught her eye, eleven cassettes in all. Most of them were labeled, but three weren't.

She took the three unlabeled cassettes to the TV/VCR. The first one she put in showed no picture. She searched for the AV channel.

Zack, waiting at the gas station by the pay phone, kept checking the road. No vehicles came; no long gray pickup hove over the horizon. He grew more and more anxious. What a harebrained idea, letting

Bitsey go back there alone! How was he going to explain this if something happened to her? He paced.

Dusty Wright's VCR and TV had different controls from the one Bitsey had at home. She had to spend valuable minutes studying the control boxes and trying various combinations of TV/VCR and base channels. She got it working. What was on the rolling tape flashed onto the screen. It was an old TV Western recorded off TV. She started to fast-forward to see if there was something later in the tape, but she quickly realized she wouldn't be able to do so with each tape. She hit EJECT.

She checked the clock: 5:32.

She inserted another unlabeled tape and hit play. It was a home video of a town meeting right-to-life debate. "Shit!" Bitsey said, hitting EJECT. She grabbed the third unlabeled tape and stuck it in.

Zack paced in front of the phone booth. He checked the road, then his watch. He had a bad feeling about all of this. Time was running out, any way you cut it. If they were really on to something that could save Gale's butt, they'd better produce it *now*. Half an hour from now would be worse than pointless.

His apprehension was ratcheting ever higher, the muscles in his neck tightening like tent cables. He stretched his neck this way and that, praying for the pickup to appear so he could call and flag Bitsey. No pickup. No traffic of any kind.

The third unlabeled tape was an *Antiques Roadshow* compilation taped from a PBS channel. Bitsey hit EJECT.

She started popping in some of the labeled tapes.

One entitled *Lucy* was an old *I Love Lucy* episode. Eject!

She grabbed another labeled *Blood on the Moon*. Play: end credits rolled for a vintage Western. "Shit!" Bitsey said again. Eject!

She shoved in another, this one hand-labeled *Death*. Maybe, maybe . . . She hit PLAY. And groaned. It was a contemporary comedy called *Death Came Suddenly*. Eject!

At the gas station phone booth, Zack's heart leapt into his mouth. Far down the curving road, he saw lights winding toward him though the gathering fog. He jumped into the phone booth, dropped two coins, and dialed six numbers. He hesitated before dialing the seventh, his finger poised as he checked the on-coming lights. As it hit the straightaway half a mile down, he could see that the approaching vehicle was a car, not the Cowboy's pickup. He quickly hung up the phone, swearing.

He mopped sweat off his face and kicked the side of the phone booth.

At Dusty's cabin, Bitsey was frantic. She had already been there too many minutes. She ran to a front window to look down the entrance road. Empty. She ran back and keyed up another tape: an old Johnny Carson interview with Pavarotti. "Shit!" Bitsey said. "Shit! Shit!" She ejected and grabbed another one hand-labeled *Tall Ships*. Who knew? She stuck it in. . . .

Zack was so anxious he was bouncing up and down by the door to the phone booth, kicking up gravel and dust. "Come on," Zack said. "Fucking come on." He moaned and hugged himself as he watched the road. Watchful waiting was not his forte.

Tall Ships was about the building of three-masted brigantines. Bitsey gave a little scream of frustration and punched it out.

Next she watched what looked like an ACLU office party—Dusty had once worked for the ACLU. She slid in another tape—the last. *Cheyenne Autumn* it said on the label in block printing, but that could be a disguising title, or it could be an old tape used for the new purpose. The movie *Cheyenne Autumn* came up on the screen. She hit EJECT and sighed in disappointment.

She got up, unsure what to do next. She went back to the bookshelf, pulled out books to look behind them for more tapes, indifferent to the mess she was making. There was nothing behind the books. She crossed the room and rifled through the drawers of a filing cabinet. Nothing but files.

She stood up and looked around the room. She saw something her eyes had passed right over before. She went to a large oak desk with an old typewriter on it. She pulled open the deep side drawers and pushed stuff around: papers, flashlight batteries, pens, tools, extension cords. No VCR tapes.

After the side drawers, she looked in the lap drawer. It was empty except for a large padded envelope addressed:

Bitsey Bloom
News Magazine
40 W. 43rd St.
New York, New York 10036

She could feel her heart pounding against her chest as she stared in disbelief. She ripped the mailer open, pulled out a VHS cassette, and checked the label: *Constance.*

The phone rang, startling her.

She looked at the phone, then at the clock: 5:41.

The phone didn't ring again. She waited a moment in the absolute silence of the cabin. Then she lunged for the VCR. She jammed the tape in, hands shaking. After a few seconds of blank static, a picture appeared: Constance standing in her kitchen by the sink, dressed in a bathrobe. Constance—very much alive—wearing the kitchen gloves and filling a glass with water.

Bitsey sat flat on the floor in front of the TV, transfixed, hyperaware of every detail she was seeing.

"Ready?" the voice of Constance said, looking toward the camera, her voice weak. The response was silence; she nodded back. She bit her lower lip and hesitated a moment. Then in one quick movement she took the key from the handcuffs and swallowed it down with the water. It went down with difficulty. She coughed, then signaled she was okay. She put the glass in the sink.

Bitsey was absolutely wide-eyed, seeing the verification of her theory unfold.

Constance took the roll of duct tape, ripped off a long section, stuck one end to the back of her gloved hand. She tore off another, smaller section and dropped the roll on the floor. She taped the smaller section over her mouth.

She then took the plastic bag from the counter, and looked at it for a beat. She turned toward the camera, mouth taped, eyes watering. She nodded once and turned back. She quickly put the bag over her head. After she had smoothed out the excess air with one hand, she took the duct tape from the other. She sealed the bag around her own neck.

She smoothly took off the gloves. They were inside out and she snapped them so that the fingers extended. She dropped them upside down on the dish rack.

She removed her robe—she was naked—and tossed it aside. It landed in the bottom right-hand corner of the screen.

Bitsey put her hand to her chest. She could not believe she was seeing this. Her heart was pounding wildly. She was trembling.

On the tape, Constance felt for the handcuffs on the counter, found them, and picked them up. She sat on the floor and, with some difficulty, snapped them on her wrists behind her back. She rolled onto her side and lay perfectly still, waiting.

Bitsey, until that moment deeply engrossed, felt the spell break as she came to the part of the tape she'd seen before—a hundred times. Averting her eyes this time, she fast-forwarded past where Constance struggled to the point where she died. Bitsey released the button and let the tape continue at normal speed.

At first, nothing happened. Constance lay perfectly still. Then a man wearing gloves walked into the frame. It was Dusty.

Bitsey practically jumped to her feet. Yes! This was it! Exactly what she'd needed.

Dusty moved over to Constance, kneeled, and removing a glove, checked her pulse. He looked briefly up and into the camera, with eyes that were a strange mixture of distraught and resigned, grief-stricken but at the same instant clench-jaw determined. He stood. He picked up Constance's robe and walked back past the tripod. For another moment Constance's dead body was the only thing on the screen. Then it went black.

A hand grabbed Bitsey's shoulder. She screamed and spun around. It was Zack, breathing hard.

"He didn't show!" Zack said. "Fuckin' move!"

Bitsey hit the EJECT button and grabbed the tape. They made a dash for the door. They banged out of the cabin, looking all around fearfully as they bounded off the porch—no pickup, no Dusty. They ran into the woods, looking back, expecting to see the pickup come charging up the entrance drive.

As they disappeared into the trees, however, nothing happened. No pickup appeared.

Then a figure stirred in the late-afternoon shadows.

Dusty stepped out from beneath the eave at the side of the house where he had been standing, watching. He shook his head with a kind of rue. Checking the time on his pocket watch, he walked slowly into the cabin where he went straight to the CD player and hit PLAY. He sat in his rocker as the soothing, tragic strains of Puccini's "Nessun Dorma"—"No man shall sleep" from *Turandot*—filled his cabin, and he closed his eyes.

Chapter 34

In the amber-tiled open shower next to the lethal injection room, David Gale enjoyed a final contemplative moment. As the hot, tension-easing water splashed his face, his arms, his back, he thought of Constance, of their heartbreaking first and last embrace, and of her courage. Her physical act took so much more iron than what he was about to go through. She had to do what had to be the hardest human act: take her own life. He had only to submit. He took strength from her example and her character—and her belief in him.

He raised his face into the spray of hot water and devoted the rest of the life of his mind and memory to images of his son:

Jamie screaming in happiness on the high-arcing backyard swing that David had strung for him from the towering silver maple.

Jamie at age two escaping from the bath and running down the sidewalk naked, laughing hysterically, his father hot on his tail.

Jamie at the Jeep the last time he saw him, crying, "Wear me like a fur, Daddy! Wear me like a fur!"

David wondered why, among all the philosophers he had read in all his years of study, none had thought to point out that one of the powerful and simple goods of a man's life—one that tells him what a man is and what his heart is capable of—is a little boy excitedly calling him Daddy. Jamie had been a blessing. To love him into his adulthood would have been to return the blessing. Absent that chance, he willed a blessing to the boy's spirit: that he somehow know his real father; that he grow up with some genetic memory in his bones of passed-along strength and character. He would go to his sleep with a father's stubborn belief that Jamie would inherit the right to be proud to be David Gale's son.

Near enough to feel the spray, the tie-down team waited patiently and dispassionately, always watching.

Bitsey ran the rental car at warp speed, roaring along the lonely country highway leading from Dusty's remote cabin. She pushed the car as fast as it and the deepening fog would allow. She was almost in tears, yelling. "Call everyone!" she said. "New York, the warden, the governor, the goddamn Supreme Court death clerk! How far is it?"

The overheat light was flickering on and off.

Zack, Bitsey's purse in his lap, ripped a page out of her phone book. "We've got eight minutes, maybe more," Zack said.

"We'll make it," Bitsey said. She was aware the engine overheat light was on. She'd been watching it from the minute they left the bowling alley parking lot below the Cowboy's cabin.

Bitsey looped up onto the high-speed interstate as one leg of the route back to town. As they came abreast of the Huntsville Motel, Bitsey swerved onto the shoulder, braked almost to a stop—and Zack, per instructions, piled out and slammed the door behind him. Bitsey was back up to speed in seconds and closing fast with the get-off onto the county spur into Huntsville.

Zack stumbled as he jumped from the moving car, caught his balance, and ran across the frontage road toward the motel through the fog. He motored, pumping his arms and legs like a sprinter. This was no time for a cool-guy lope. He went flat out, leaving nothing in the tank, his phone list in one hand, the motel key in the other, spit flying from his open mouth.

Back in the holding cell, David sat on his bed eating his last meal from a tray on his lap.

He was dressed in a blue oxford button-down shirt and chinos, the kind of outfit a college prof would wear on his day off. He had shaved for the occasion.

Just outside his cell, perched uncomfortably on prison chairs, sat the warden and chaplain eating duplicate meals. The warden and chaplain held themselves ready to chat, ready to make conversation should the condemned man desire—as sometimes in his sweating, mounting terror he did. It was the prisoner's choice.

In this case, silence was the prisoner's choice. Prisoner Gale had said all he was going to say in this life, apparently, and chose not to communicate further.

The only sounds were the clicking of the men's plastic knives and forks, as they ate strawberries with whipped cream and chocolate shavers.

As Bitsey whipped the rental car down off the interstate onto the county two lane, she swore, starting to panic. She had not yet reached the Huntsville outskirts and the overheat light was now full on, no longer flickering but bright red and steady. Bitsey glared at it, then turned on the radio. A country & western song played. She punched the scan button. "Give me the time," Bitsey shouted at the radio. "Give me the goddamn time!"

She was getting close. She flew past a sign indicating that the TDCJ Huntsville Unit was three miles ahead. The sign disappeared behind her into the fog. She pushed harder on the accelerator—she had to fly, time was draining away. She smelled something. And at the same time saw it—smoke.

"It's time to go."

True to his word, the chaplain had pronounced the runic phrase.

David's cell door was opened. He was led out into the hallway. The chaplain and the special three-man tie-down squad escorted him from his cell the five paces to the green door at the end of the room. The door was marked only with the number seventeen. He stopped at a table before the door, and a guard poured him an orange juice, which he downed in one big swallow.

On the foggy county two lane, Bitsey's heart sank. The smell of burning was sharper, worse. Smoke was seeping from the cracks around the hood and up through the floorboard. The engine was making indescribable noises of stress.

Abruptly the engine seized, the pistons, their lubricant burned away, superheated, swelled and froze in their cylinders. The rental car jerked, then clunked to a dead roll, now a powerless shell with wheels, a lump of solidly fused metal for an engine.

Bitsey jumped out, VHS cassette in hand. Without bothering to close the car door, she took off sprinting along the road like a hundred-meter dasher, running all out. She raced along between the crop stubble and scrawny cows in the bordering fields. Seconds counted. This was the test of her life, she was agonizingly aware.

Across the brown fields, a mile-long goods train rolled along slowly, seeming to keep pace with her.

Emotions sometimes ran high at executions—it depended on the notoriety of the condemned, the nature of his crime, the clearness or questionability of his guilt. This particular state-sponsored killing—some viewed it as a human sacrifice on the alter of tidy-society fundamentalists—was eliciting sharp emotional responses on both sides of the death penalty issue.

Hence the news chopper hovering above the crowd, now numbering several hundred, outside the Huntsville Unit. The local TV news director thought it a nice possibility that the protesters would produce some usable footage before the tribal rite was over.

The gable clock read 5:56.

A tower guard looked down on the assemblage, keeping a wary eye out.

Protestors chanted at either end of the blocked-off section directly in front of the Death House entrance. Journalists packed the press section across the street with their elaborate television remote equipment and satellite uplinks. The area within the roadblock was jammed with nervous police and technical people keeping watch on both groups of protesters. If there were to be a riot, they would be right in the middle of it.

Donna Wells, a female TV reporter, was psyching herself up, rehearsing her stand-up before a video camera and crew, with the so-far-quiet doors of the Huntsville Unit behind her. Sharing with the rest of the media corps present the conviction that it was not a matter of if but when, she had just one speech prepared: "As you can see behind me," she said, "lawyer Braxton Belyeu is leaving the prison, signifying that the execution of David Gale is over. Belyeu was Gale's only witness because he was a totally fucked-up guy who killed his friends. How's my key light?"

Donna was practicing among a row of other reporters all doing the same thing—polishing their spontaneous, live-with-breaking-news comments—while waiting for their cue to perform the news.

Her key light was fine, Donna's operator told her. "But you're getting shiny."

"I am?" she said, casting an annoyed look at the still-closed doors of the Huntsville Unit as if to say, Can we move here, people?

She yelled down the row, "Does anyone have any powder?"

Bitsey had put the rental car out of sight in a few seconds, tearing along the fogged-in country road. Visibility was no more than fifty yards. The sounds of her breathing and shoes hitting the pavement echoed in the mist.

Sundowner birdcalls drifted faintly across the brown fields. Yard dogs in the houses on the out-skirts of town set up a flurry of yapping as she went pounding by.

She crossed the town line into Huntsville, making a dash through small-town America, getting ever closer to the prison.

At one end of the embargoed area fronting the Huntsville Unit, a religious woman with two small children pled to a cop across the barrier. "When Cain killed Abel, God cast him out," the religious woman said. "He didn't kill him!" The cop, an old-timer for whom this scene was as ancient and ritualistic as a kabuki dance, looked at the woman without even seeing her. He moved back and forth, looking for the real crazy who might want to shoot somebody to protest—or endorse—state killing.

Not far now, less than a mile distant from the prison, a car appeared out of the fog and came up quickly behind Bitsey as she ran. Its horn blared. She turned, intent on waving it down. The driver leaned on his horn, swerved around her, and drove on.

At the barriers, a woman from the "anti" crowd threw a plastic bottle. A cop ran over to arrest her. As a scuffle developed and a few placards were thrown, the TV chopper wheeled and got the "news" on camera live. His news director back at the local station was pleased; the expense of dispatching the chopper was justified.

Bitsey ran through the mist-cloaked Huntsville town square. The prison was close, the towers of the Walls faintly visible, rising in the fog over other buildings.

In the media pen outside at the Huntsville Unit, a French radio reporter looked askance at the protesters and the carnival of TV reporters and their elaborate gear. "This," he said to an American colleague, "could never happen in France. It's barbaric."

True, thought the American journalist. It's been years since you guys beheaded your entire government.

Bitsey dashed hard past a run-down gas station, a vacant lot, a diner.

Inside the diner, a second-unit news crew was getting some man-in-the-street wallpaper to hang behind the main, on-scene execution story.

"Personally, I think it's not hard enough for him," a waitress told a news crew. "He just gets stuck in the arm and goes to sleep. He should suffer like she did."

The scuffle at the Huntsville Unit anti–death penalty barricade continued. The cop struggled to pull the bottle-thrower over the sawhorse. The "pro" group joined the shouting. "Strap her down, too!" "Murderers must die!" "Murderers must die!"

*   *   *

Bitsey cut down a residential street that led toward the Huntsville Unit, just a few blocks away. She hadn't dared look at her watch for some time. The sounds of chanting protestors over the streets encouraged her. Please, please, not too late . . .

The glass double doors of the Huntsville Unit swung briskly open. Grover and Belyeu came out of the doors to meet the flash of cameras.

Grover had on his official self-important face, neither glad nor gloomy, just: I've got the goods. Come listen at my feet.

Belyeu was his usual picture of slightly sardonic detachment.

The gable clock on the wall read 6:17.

In the Huntsville sports bar where Bitsey and Zack had taken a meal, a good-looking buzz-cut blond youth draped in a booth said to a journalist, "Mister, we're just like any other small town in America. God's truth."

His buddies in the booth readied their own sound bites. They'd seen this kind of stuff on TV. Now it was their turn.

"Will this be on at eleven?" one of the kids said.

On a TV over the counter, a live news report of the scene at the prison was airing. Shots of the protesters, the media bedlam, the death chamber were intercut with file tape of David Gale and Constance Harraway making death penalty pronouncements: "Ever since the world began," Constance said to a hearing at the state capitol, "a procession of the weak, the poor, and the helpless has filled prisons and been put to death in the name of justice."

"Nothing is more cruel," David was seen saying at the same hearing, "than righteous indignation. This is not justice but a bloodlust, a need for revenge."

Bitsey, breathing hoarsely, exhausted, pounded along the sidewalk. She was close, almost within sight of the Walls. The sounds coming from there, in her jumbled, chaotic brain, gave flickers of hope, then a flash of dread.

In Austin, at the DeathWatch office, Josh, Rosie, Beth, and others all sat quietly, feeling puny and alone. No conversation passed among them. The awful circumstance was too freighted with misery and horror.

Silent tears welled in Beth's eyes as Constance came on a TV, file tape on a news feed live from Huntsville: "We teach people to kill and the state is the one that teaches them," Constance said. "If a state wishes that its citizens respect human life, then the state should stop killing."

The ironies in this case were extreme, noted the live-on-scene reporter as she introduced a piece of tape of David standing outside the Huntsville Unit giving an interview. "Capital punishment," he said, "is banned in every civilized country but the United States—not just because it debases our humanity, but because it has no effect whatsoever in stopping murder."

Rosie couldn't look at the TV. She stared down at her desk, tapping a red Magic Marker on her phone-list pad.

"Nothing cheapens human life as much as war," Gale said, "and in peace nothing debases human life as much as killing by the state. It is not justice, it is cowardice."

Josh, David's greatest fan and emulator, squeezed his fists to contain fury of the kind reserved for gods who fail.

Outside Welcome House at Huntsville, a tumult: reporters shouted questions at Belyeu and Duke Grover, TV news performers did their stand-ups, video crews shouted directions and cursed each other for fouling their sight lines, on-scene producers watched their monitors and cued talent.

On the monitors were reruns of pronouncements from David and Constance at earlier high-profile executions:

"The United States is the only constitutional democracy that permits the execution of the mentally retarded and child offenders," David said on a CNN archive tape. "The killers of white victims are four times more likely to receive the death penalty. We continue the slaughter of the poor and the disadvantaged, but morality is never upheld by legalized murder."

Noting that Gale must have been gratified to learn it, the CNN in-studio anchor discussed the Supreme Court's recent ruling that executing the mentally retarded was unconstitutionally cruel. The execution of juveniles was death penalty opponents' next Supreme Court target, he said, with eighty-three youthful offenders currently awaiting execution across the country.

Constance's voice came from another monitor: "In

a civilized society," she said, "we rightly shed tears for the victims, but it doesn't mean that we should continue the cruelty. Shouldn't we be above that? If our hearts are compassionate for the dead, why should they be brutalized toward the living?"

From the sound, Bitsey was practically in the midst of the media bedlam and protestor chanting. She turned a corner and saw the lighted circus through the fog a half block away. At the same instant, something caught her eye off to the left, at a side exit from the Walls.

She slowed dramatically, reflexively clutching the videocassette to her chest.

A Texas Department of Corrections ambulance, its lights flashing jarringly through the fog, came slowly out the prison exit. There was no siren, only the sound of chanting from in front of the Huntsville Unit half a block away.

For Bitsey everything decelerated to nightmare slow motion.

She came to a stop, breathing heavily, terror seizing her heart. She watched the ambulance roll out of the prison and turn toward the vacant field behind, and she knew she was too late.

She screamed and fell to her knees on the grass verge, wailing. No one heard. The noise of the media circus drowned out her cries.

She sobbed in exhaustion, watching the ambulance lights recede into the fog. Images pierced her brain: the open and unmarked grave that awaited across the field, she knew, in a dirt-patch burial ground; grave markers that had no names, only numbers. She knew that David Gale's heart had been stopped and that soon he would be slid silently into that hole in the ground. That the chaplain would recite rote words with only the warden and inmate gravediggers present. That the diggers would tidy up the wound in the earth and everybody would turn and go back to life, and the "elimination" of David Gale would be accomplished.

And that she had hopelessly, pathetically failed.

Chapter 35

At the DeathWatch office in the Texas state capital, Rosie got up and crossed to the picture wall. She made a red X over the photo of David Gale. She sat back tiredly at her desk and put her head in her hands and wept.

At his cabin in the woods, Dusty Wright sat in silence with his pocket watch in his hand, watching the second hand sweep around and around. No music. No sounds at all.

When the time for the execution had come and gone, he stood up, put away his watch, and walked to the table by the front door. He picked up a wallet case from the table and shoved it in his pocket. He leaned down and picked up a good-sized suitcase. He turned and looked once around the cabin. He stuck his Stetson on his head and walked out the front door, locking it behind him.

Behind him in the house, in the middle of his big wooden desk, sat the radiator cap from the rental car.

Braxton Belyeu entered the Austin Municipal Airport at an hour he considered obscene in its earliness.

Worn out from the proceedings at Huntsville the day before, the interviews that dragged on into the evening, the late drive back, Belyeu nonetheless moved with purpose; his job was not finished. He made his way past the ticket counters on the departures floor and strode on toward the security gates. He was carrying the aluminum suitcase Bitsey had delivered to his office.

Belyeu walked past an airport bar. On the swivel TV above the bartender, CNN reporter A. J. Roberts appeared over a BREAKING NEWS caption.

"Here's what we know so far," Roberts said to the camera. "Last night, *NEWS Magazine* posted on their Web site a video obtained by reporter Bitsey Bloom. . . ."

Belyeu paused, listened to a few seconds of the report, and walked away—as though none of it were news to him.

Other travelers listened transfixed as Roberts continued. "The footage appeared to show Constance Harraway committing suicide. Bloom reports that she received the tape Friday morning at a motel in Huntsville, where she was staying while conducting Gale's last interview. The tape apparently had been in the possession of a former DeathWatch employee"—Roberts read the name off a card—"Dustin Emil Wright."

Belyeu heard the same report airing on other TVs as he continued down the concourse. As he glanced at one in passing, he caught a glimpse of footage of Dusty's woodside cabin near Huntsville, swarming with cops.

"As you can see," Roberts said, "police have been in and out of his cabin all morning, looking for clues to his whereabouts."

Belyeu strode on.

*   *   *

On the twelfth floor at 40 West Forty-third in New York, *NEWS Magazine*'s editorial offices, Bitsey watched the banks of TVs along with a dozen colleagues.

Kruger stood beside her. A few people congratulated Bitsey. She attempted to smile and nod, though she didn't look away from the TV. Kruger shushed the others to listen to the same A. J. Roberts report playing in the airport in Austin.

"The footage appears to show Constance Harraway committing suicide," reporter Roberts said.

Zack watched Bitsey from the other side of the room. She looked over at him, then quickly looked back to the TV.

"The tape apparently had been in the possession of a former DeathWatch employee . . ." Roberts said, reporting from in front of Dusty's cabin. Other journalists and gawkers milled around the woodsy place. Police vehicles were visible. Suits and officers moved in and out of the cabin. Roberts read the name from a card: "Dustin Emil Wright,"

Similar interviews and vignettes played on all the TV screens around the room, as saturation coverage of the unfolding David Gale story gathered steam, stranger and more mesmerizing with each new development.

Out of sight of the media, the story went on. Attorney Belyeu walked into a men's room at the far end of the departures concourse at the Austin airport, carrying the aluminum suitcase. He walked to a row of sinks, set the bag on the floor, and started to wash his hands. To his left, a businessman with two sample cases combed his hair. Belyeu looked in the mirror and saw Dusty coming out of a stall.

Dusty Wright, said the CNN reporter on-screen at *NEWS Magazine* headquarters, was ". . . a fanatic in the movement to stop the death penalty. It appears Wright withheld the tape to make an obscure point about the potential for error in capital punishment cases."

Bitsey watched, trying to contain her emotions. All the other staffers watched, too. Zack, though, watched her. She looked in his direction. He smiled sadly and looked away.

In the Austin airport men's room, Dusty moved over from the toilet stall and washed his hands next to Belyeu. He looked down at the aluminum suitcase.

The businessman picked up his sample cases and left.

"All there?" Dusty said.

"Passport and ticket as well," Belyeu said.

Dusty splashed water on his face and looked at Belyeu. Then at himself—at his own weary eyes.

The slick, car-salesman governor of Texas, Bob Hardin, dominated the TV screens at 40 West Forty-third. He was at a podium in front of the capitol building in Austin, surrounded by journalists.

"It's a terrible tragedy, and I assure you there will be a full investigation," Governor Hardin said. "I assure you that this man Dusty Wright will be caught and shown swift justice."

He showed his deeply felt remorse for the terrible tragedy with a reflective pause.

"But the people of Texas," he said, "are not deterred. We are still solidly behind the death penalty because it works—the system cannot be blamed for the acts of one deranged individual with an ax to grind. Hey, let's not throw the baby out with the bathwater, people."

Kruger snorted and said to Bitsey, "Capital punishment approval rates dropped seventeen points in the overnights," Kruger said.

"Great, now only eighty-three percent of the state supports it," Zack said softly.

Bitsey just looked at the TV, trying to make it through.

Dusty patted his face dry, then bent down and picked up the aluminum suitcase from the floor of the men's room. He had a feeling he'd better be on his way. Thankfully, no photographs of him had yet made their way to the TV screens, though he had heard his name. He stood tall and turned from the mirror.

Belyeu adjusted the knot on his tie. "What are you going to do?" he said.

"Go to the opera," Dusty said. He nodded to the attorney, walking past him and out the door.

Belyeu watched him disappear—complex, prickly, contradictory, impossible individual that he was. What strange paths we take in life and what strange roles we are called upon to play, he thought. How pathetically inadequate was the rule of law in untangling the webs human beings weave. Please, Fate, he prayed, let that odd duck get on the plane and out of here before the shit storm descends.

On many of the twelve or so TVs around the editorial floor at *NEWS Magazine*, file footage ran of David being led in chains from an Austin jailhouse to a waiting van for his murder arraignment.

Over that tape, that now had a meaning 180 degrees reversed from when it originally aired, A. J. Roberts concluded the Huntsville report: "Of course, the ultimate irony is that David Gale, a man who became an unwitting martyr, may achieve in death what he worked for but could not accomplish in life." In the file footage, David wore the same clothes he had worn into the execution chamber.

Bitsey watched, unable not to, biting her lower lip in a manner reminiscent of Constance.

Roberts signed off, "This is A. J. Roberts in Bastrop, Texas," and threw the news to Aaron Brown at the CNN broadcast studios in Atlanta.

Brown went to a tribute segment, letting run without commentary a compilation of David Gale and Constance Harraway sound bites pulled off Internet sources and out of their own archives:

"Throughout history, brutal public executions were never a deterrent," David said, reading a statement at Senate subcommittee hearings in the 1980s, just as executions were gathering steam. "You can crush a man to death, gouge out his eyes, and throw him to the lions, and it still doesn't work because fear of death never reduced crime. The death penalty just gratifies our desire for revenge, and this diminishes all of us."

"If capital punishment had worked," Constance said, speaking to a criminal law class at Duke Law School, "then there would be no more killing on our streets."

At the Southern Center for Human Rights colloquium on the power of judges to override juries in death penalty cases, Constance argued that juries, because they are not in the business of sentencing every day, tend to be more sensitive to the enormity of imposing death. "Anyone who has a grain of sympathy, compassion, kindness, and understanding," she said, "will hate and detest the taking of human life."

"Nearly every religious denomination in the U.S.," David said to Ted Koppel, "opposes the death penalty."

Chapter 36

It was clear and warm on the northeast coast of Spain when Dusty flew in and took a taxi ride up along the Camino Real before his evening appointments.

It was his good fortune that on that same day, Puccini was being performed at the Barcelona Opera House—not just Puccini but *Turandot*, his favorite. He was in love with the melodious arias and emotional choruses, and much taken too with the idea that this was Puccini's swan song—his great final offering as, stricken with throat cancer, he worked on the score in a Brussels hospital until the day he died.

The Cowboy got a pricey seat in the orchestra, doffed his Stetson, and settled in. Drinking in the baroque splendors of the hall and the heart-melting love songs, he moved his head ever so slightly to the music.

At the interval, the Cowboy was quickly up and out of his seat, through the grand doors and down the front steps. He took to the street—the Ramblas—where he walked along briskly, carrying the aluminum suitcase and a duty-free bag. He was not sightseeing; he was looking for an address.

He came to a building, checked its address against a piece of paper, and turned in at the entrance.

In the interior of the ornate and handsomely maintained old building, he avoided the elevator and mounted the stairs to an upper floor. There he walked along the carpeted hallway, looking at the door numbers. At number six, he paused—and turned as an old Spanish woman passed him. He took a photograph of Sharon Gale from his pocket and held it up to her. *"Señora esta viviendo aqui?"* he said.

"Sí," the old Spanish woman said. *"Sí."*

"Gracias," Dusty said.

The old woman gave him a suspicious look and moved down the stairs.

Dusty took David's Yale sweatshirt out of the duty-free bag and laid it over the aluminum suitcase. He rang the doorbell at number six, turned, and walked back down the hall. He stood at the top of the stairs, waiting for someone to answer before he descended.

Sharon, older now, not untouched by the strains of life even here in her Iberian love nest, opened the door and saw the sweatshirt. She looked up and down the hall and stepped out, looking down toward the stairs. There was no one to be seen; Dusty was gone.

Dusty was back in his seat at the Opera House in time for the rest of *Turandot*. Greatly relieved, unburdened, he was able to lose himself in the drama and let his heart calm down. He moved a hand in time to the music.

*   *   *

Bitsey sat at her neurotically neat desk, looking out the window at life up and down West Forty-third Street. It was a sunny day in New York and the human race was out in force.

She was dressed down for once, not the power figure she felt she always had to be. UnBitseylike, her mind was wandering; her focus had not been so keen since the debacle in Texas.

Framed on her cubicle wall was the latest *NEWS Magazine* cover: a photo of David with the headline: THE LIFE OF DAVID GALE. The smug pleasure she usually experienced on pulling off a journalistic coup was missing. She was emotionally flatlining.

A shaved-bald mail guy pushing a cart and wearing latex gloves dropped a FedEx package on her desk. "This just came," he said.

She looked down at the oversized, bulging mailer and read:

Belyeu & Crane
420 Congress Ave
Austin, Texas 78710

She stared at it, puzzled, turned it over, hefted it. Then opened it. She pulled out Cloud Dog, the stuffed sheep, and a handwritten note on Belyeu & Crane stationary.

David wanted you to have this. He said it would be the key to your freedom.

Regards,
Braxton Belyeu

*   *   *

Guillermo, a Spanish yuppie with a thriving American import business, sat reading the newspaper, waiting for Sharon to finish what she was doing and make him his cocktail.

Jamie was obediently holed up in his room; children at cocktail hour in this Spanish household were better loved absent than underfoot. Jamie was happily IM-ing with his international school friends, in Spanish, about Spanish girls, European World Cup soccer minutiae, French girls, a cool new Dave Matthews Band bootleg CD, and Italian girls.

Guillermo watched Sharon open the suitcase. Inside, there were stacks of bills—not Euros, dollars. Guillermo raised an interested eyebrow.

Sharon's eyes went wide for an instant, then narrowed at the sight of a postcard sitting on top of the money. She picked it up: a picture of San Francisco on the front. She flipped it over. The back was addressed to David Gale at his apartment address in Austin. The handwritten message read, "I'm sorrier than you can know—Berlin, the student who would do anything."

Sharon stared coolly at the message. She recognized instantly the point of David's sending it to her; she got it. And she got the point of the money, knew for whom it was intended.

She was uncomfortably aware that her ex-husband had just been executed. She thought that she knew the whole story and was intensely bitter to have been tarred by association with it. She knew only a fraction of the story. She was soon to hear a great deal more—about a different David from the one she had divorced.

And Jamie, if not soon, then in a few years, would

hear from a source other than his mother about the father he barely remembered, and the man his father was.

Dusty, not far away enjoying *Turandot* at the Opera House, closed his eyes as the music built. By the time the little Chinese girl Liu martyred herself, died because she loved, tears ran unashamedly down the Cowboy's creased face. He cried for Constance and for himself. It would be a long time before he could go home to Texas.

At her desk in her cubicle, Bitsey held the stuffed sheep and looked at the note, puzzled. "Key to your freedom?" she said. "Key to your . . ."

Suddenly the dots connected and she understood. She squeezed the sheep, shook it, heard something. She grabbed for her scissors and cut Cloud Dog open along the seam in the belly. A VHS tape was in the stuffing. It was hand-labeled: OFF THE RECORD.

She jumped up, swung out of her cubicle and marched past the other cubicles. She ran out of the room, past Zack, and down a hall into a multimedia room.

He watched her with curiosity and started to follow, but saw her close the door behind herself.

Bitsey locked the door and slid the tape into a VHS deck. She sat on the edge of a chair, punched on a monitor, and hit PLAY.

It was the Constance tape, but it was cued to after her death, to the moment Dusty picked up Constance's robe and walked toward the camera and past it, out of frame. The subsequent images were only of Constance's body, but the mike picked up a sound:

the opening of the sliding door to the patio, behind the camera.

"It's over," Dusty's voice called, off-screen.

A long beat, then footsteps sounded on the patio and on the kitchen floor. David walked into frame. He took a couple of steps past the camera toward Constance's body and stopped, facing her. The camera saw him only from behind. He looked at her, ran his hands over his head. He went to her and kneeled. He reached down and with his thumb gently stroked her face through the plastic. He stood, turned and walked back to the camera. He reached behind the lens to turn it off, and as he did so, his face filled two-thirds of the frame, his watery eyes looking past the lens. The other third of the frame still held Constance's body.

There was a click. The screen went black.

Bitsey sat back and watched the blank staticky tape roll on. The realizations hit her all at once.

She had been duped.

She was free.

David Gale's death was not a terrible miscarriage of justice after all, but a suicide.

And to free her, he had put the proof of suicide in her hands. Proof that also gave her the power to destroy his—and Constance's—"martyrdoms" for their cause.

And the final flash of light. This was what David meant when he said to her, "You're not here to save me. You're here to save my son's memory of his father—that's all I want."

The tape in her hands was the last full measure of a father's love.

She gazed out the window at the people down

below going on with their lives, tied up in the ordinary, struggling. But they all had tomorrows; tomorrows tended to come wrapped in hope.

Would she release the tape?

Maybe she would—someday. After the cause was accomplished.

Or maybe, when his son was older, she would leave it up to him.

She went out to join the hordes walking on West Forty-third Street, feeling pretty alive.

Epilogue

The Reverend Stephen Lipman resigned as Huntsville's Death House chaplain two days after David Gale's execution.

The Warden at the San Quentin Death House in San Francisco, along with several of his chaplains and security officers, handed in their resignations in the weeks following Gale's execution.

Wardens and chaplains at death houses in Florida and Alabama walked away from their jobs.

In June 2002, the U.S. Supreme Court banned executions of the mentally retarded, generally defined as having an I.Q. of seventy or lower.

The ruling occasioned elation by abolitionists—"A great victory for human rights," a defendant's lawyer said.

"In the future we may look at this case as a turning point in reform of the death penalty in general," said an ACLU official, noting a growing movement away from the death penalty in state legislatures.

Pro–death penalty voices predicted a glut of litigation on behalf of convicted killers. "All of a sudden everybody on death row is going to become retarded," said a Mississippi attorney general.

"I bet I could score a fifty-nine if my life depended on it," said a Virginia county Commonwealth's attorney.

"Any death row inmate who does not file an appeal to have himself declared retarded ought to have his I.Q. tested," said a spokesperson for Justice For All, a Texas victims' rights group.

While all-out assaults on the death penalty have failed in the U. S., the recent salami-slicer strategy of the abolitionists is working. The execution of minors is the next target of anti–death penalty activists.

The only nations in the world that still execute juvenile offenders are Iran, Pakistan, Saudi Arabia, Nigeria, and the United States.

In July 2002, a bipartisan vote of the Senate Judiciary Committee passed the Innocence Protection Act, a bill to prevent the execution of innocent defendants by providing Federal money for better lawyers for poor defendants and DNA testing for all death row inmates.

In July 2002, U.S. District Court Judge Jed S. Rakoff ruled that the current federal death penalty law is unconstitutional. The fact that twelve death row inmates, all convicted by unanimous juries, were recently cleared through DNA evidence shows, he said, that "an undue risk of executing innocent people exists," making the death penalty "tantamount to foreseeable, state-sponsored murder of innocent human beings.'' Judge Rakoff's ruling, while applying to just one case for now, is likely to influence the continuing national debate.